Girl, Barely 15: Flirting for England

ALSO BY SUE LIMB

Girl, 15, Charming but Insane
Girl, Nearly 16: Absolute Torture
Girl, Going on 17: Pants on Fire

Girl, Barely 15: Flirting for England

Sue Limb

DELACORTE PRESS

Published by Delacorte Press
an imprint of Random House Children's Books
a division of Random House, Inc.
New York

Delacorte Press and colophon are registered trademarks of Random House, Inc.

Visit us on the Web!
www.randomhouse.com/teens

Educators and librarians, for a variety of teaching tools,
visit us at www.randomhouse.com/teachers

Library of Congress Cataloging-in-Publication Data is available upon request.

ISBN: 978-0-385-73538-4 (trade)   ISBN: 978-0-385-90520-6 (lib. bdg.)

The text of this book is set in 11-point Palatino.

Printed in the United States of America

10 9 8 7 6 5 4 3 2

Random House Children's Books supports the First Amendment
and celebrates the right to read.

To Liliane Binnie (née Sanchez),
my French pen pal, still a good friend after all these years

Dear Edouard,
    . . . or may I call you Ed? Edouard is
so . . . it sounds a bit . . .

Oh no! Insulting him already! Being rude about his name! Jess screwed up the piece of paper and threw it at the bin. It missed.

Dear Edouard,
    You're my French exchange partner . . .

He knows that already, retardo! Jess screwed up the piece of paper and threw it at the bin. It missed.

Dear Edouard,
Hi! My name's Jess Jordan and apparently we're ex-
change partners . . .

"Apparently"? As if it had all happened by accident and Jess was a bit embarrassed about it? And would, to be honest, have preferred to exchange with a monkey?

Jess screwed up the piece of paper and also screwed up her eyes, her fists, and her toes and uttered a strangled cry of anguish. Why was this so damn difficult? She looked out of the window. It was raining. Mustn't mention that. French people probably thought it rained in England all the time.

If only she hadn't got herself into this mess. A couple of weeks ago, the French teacher Mrs. Bailey had said she had "an announcement to make about the forthcoming French exchange scheme." She'd looked awkward.

"Things are a bit unusual this year," she'd said, "because there are more French boys wanting to take part than English boys. So I'm afraid some of you girls will have to have a French boy as your exchange partner. Put your hand up if you don't mind."

Jess's arm had shot up so fast, she'd almost dislocated her shoulder. A French boy! What could be more sexy? Jess was dazzled by the thought of all those French footballers with their shiny brown eyes and pouty French lips.

But now, trying to write her first letter to the guy, she was *so* wishing she hadn't. If only Edouard had been a girl, Jess could easily have dashed off a letter introducing herself, no problem. But now she felt self-conscious. She had to come across as attractive, charismatic, and mysterious, even if her country *was* saturated with rain.

Dear Edouard,

I'm your French exchange partner. I'm sorry I have to write in English, as my French is totally useless. My name's Jess Jordan and I live in a loft-style apartment overlooking twinkling skyscrapers. My mum is descended from the Royal House of Portugal. Her name is Joanna the Slightly Mad. My dad lives in Hollywood. He's a film producer. I was born on a stormy night in July, when it rained rubies . . .

So much for fiction. Jess screwed up the paper. It missed the bin. OK, there was only one way of doing this. She had to imagine Edouard was a girl—even call him by a girl's name, and then just change the name back to Edouard afterwards.

Dear Josephine,

Hi! I'm your French exchange partner. My name's Jess Jordan. I hope you don't mind if I write in English. It's OK if you write back in French, because my mum understands it. She's a librarian. We live in an old terraced house, not far from the park.

My dad's an artist and he lives miles away, by the sea. My parents split up years ago but Dad and I talk loads on the phone and send each other texts and e-mails. I see him when he comes up to town.

I don't have any brothers and sisters, which is OK, but I don't have any pets either, which is a major tragedy.

I'm about average height and I've got dark hair which is just ordinary, but I have really high-class, Nobel Prize–winning dandruff.

Jess crossed out that last bit about dandruff. It sucked, trying to describe the way you looked. Mrs. Bailey had said everyone should introduce themselves by letter, and supply a photo. They had to give their letters in to Mrs. Bailey as if they were essays, and she was going to check them all before sending them off.

How totally Stone Age, thought Jess. *Everybody uses e-mail these days*. Mrs. Bailey was such a control freak.

But the horrors of trying to write the letter were nothing compared to the agony of selecting a photo. Should she send him the one where she looked like an overweight stalker? Or the cross-eyed terrorist with a headache? Neither, of course. In fact Jess had had a brilliant idea about the photo—but right now she had to get back to the freaking letter.

I like music, especially rap. I love watching TV comedy, and when I leave school I want to be a stand-up comedian. How about you?

Jess's mind went blank. Her brain stalled. She had stopped thinking of Edouard as a girl and become trapped once again in the knowledge that he was a guy.

Suddenly the phone rang. Jess threw down her pen, raced out to the kitchen, and grabbed the receiver.

"Hello?"

"Hello, dear, it's only me!" It was Granny. Jess beamed and sat down on the nearest chair.

"Granny! How are you? Tell me the latest about your exciting life! Have you been windsurfing today?"

There was a plate of grapes on the table. Jess helped herself to a few. She could hear Granny chuckling. That was good. They'd been a bit worried about Granny recently, since Grandpa died. But today she sounded quite chirpy.

"No, dear, I haven't been windsurfing today. I thought I'd try that bungee jumping instead." Jess laughed. Granny's fantasy repertoire of dangerous sports was a standing joke. "But how are you, Jess, love? Looking forward to the Easter holidays? When do you break up?"

"Oh, I don't know," said Jess. "I'm hopeless with dates and stuff. But before Easter we've got the French exchange thingy. This guy Edouard's coming to stay."

"Really, dear? A *boy*? How did you get that one past Mum?"

"Oh, it's like, she's so thrilled about him being French and stuff, and she's so looking forward to showing off her language skills, I don't think she's even sort of realized he's going to be male."

"Well, I hope he's handsome, dear."

"I haven't seen a photo of him yet," said Jess. "But with my luck, he'll have very large nostrils or perhaps a pulsating wart on his chin."

They chatted for a while about revolting men they had known. Granny's milkman, Geoff, was the World Champion in this event—though, tragically, he was unaware of his distinction. Then, after much other gossip, Granny asked to speak to Mum.

"Sorry, Mum's out," said Jess, finishing off the last of the grapes. "It's her yoga night."

"Oh yes, I should have remembered," said Granny. "What a shame! There's something I can't wait to tell her."

"Sounds exciting!" said Jess. "Tell me instead."

There was a strange, tantalizing pause.

"I'd love to, dear, but . . . I think I'd better talk to your mum about it first," said Granny.

"Well, I'm vastly intrigued," said Jess. Whatever could Granny be talking about? Could she, possibly, be dating? The period of mourning had gone on long enough. Maybe she had recruited a boy toy of, say, forty? "But I'm deeply insulted that you aren't prepared to confide in me," Jess went on.

Granny giggled.

"Sorry, dear," she said. "But it's kind of, well, a bit, well . . . I'd better talk to your mum first, that's all."

A horrid thought crossed Jess's mind. Maybe Granny was ill! Maybe the lightheartedness was all a front. She felt a sickening lurch of fear.

"Is everything all right, Granny?" she asked. "You're not ill or anything?"

"Oh no, dear, thank you," said Granny. "Quite the contrary, in fact. I'm tickety-boo. But I think perhaps I ought to ring back later. I daren't say any more now, in case I say too much and get into trouble."

"OK," said Jess. "But if you've won the lottery, don't forget I'm your only grandchild and I've inherited all your sterling qualities."

They said goodbye and Jess went back to her letter. It

seemed even more dull after her conversation with Granny, but she had to force herself back into pen pal mode.

How do you pronounce "Edouard"?

She was getting desperate now, like making small talk at a party.

One of my friends—Fred—says it's pronounced: Ed-oooooo-argh!

Insulting his name again. Still, she had really made some progress. Jess crossed out the bit about pronouncing his name and rushed on to another topic.

My best friend is Flora Barclay. She's tall and blond and gorgeous, and she's also really clever. Her dad is so rich, they go to the Caribbean for their holidays . . .

Jess crossed out the bit about Flora. What was she thinking of, talking up Flo like that? The guy was going to fall in love with her anyway the moment his shiny brown French eyes met Flora's sky blue orbs. That was what always happened when boys first clapped eyes on fabulous Flo.

She was blond, she was beautiful, and she was so *relentlessly* delightful that Jess simply had to be her best mate forever, even though it would have been far more convenient—and stylish—to hate her from afar.

Jess wrote a couple of sentences describing her school, her road, and her house. Never had a letter been so dull.

You could have had more fun reading the label on a sauce bottle.

I love fish and chips and pizza but I've heard French food is really amazing, so I'm looking forward to some stylish grub when I come over to your place next year.

Still, Edouard probably wouldn't care how boring her letter was. Once he'd set eyes on her photo, he'd be instantly under her spell. Because Jess had a plan about the photo. It couldn't be a photo of her as her real self, though: as she looked now. It would have to be, well, *digitally enhanced*.

Jess's gaze wandered to the sofa, where she had recently spent a divine three hours with *BLING!*—the ultimate celebrity magazine.

Which photo . . . Britney? Scarlett? Beyoncé? Obviously Jess wasn't just going to clip the image of a screen star out of a magazine and pretend it was her. She'd get Fred to enhance her image on his PC, mixing up her own features with those of her chosen celebs. She deeply envied Scarlett Johansson's full lips and Beyoncé's lovely eyes.

By the time gorgeous Edouard arrived in England, he'd be madly in love with her. And as long as she always stood with her back to the light, with any luck he'd never notice the difference between her photo and the real thing. Jess swiftly buried any nagging doubts, signed the letter, and put it in an envelope. She didn't seal it, though. She left it open for the photo.

The photo was still an issue. But at least she'd be getting one in return. And receiving a photo of Edouard was going to be the most important thing in the next few days.

2

$\mathcal{J}$ ess cornered Fred the next morning, the moment she got to school. She pinned him against the wall.

"Parsons, I need your help!" she hissed. "You've got to change me from a hideous minger to a screen goddess, tonight."

Fred's gray eyes flared in surprise. He shrugged his skinny shoulders and looked down at her with a saucy grin.

"What's brought this on?" he said. "I'd assumed you were Life President of the Ugly Club."

Jess punched Fred lightly in the ribs. This was part of their routine. He gasped in pain, then pulled her hair. She gasped in pain. They could now resume their conversation.

"Why is a makeover necessary?" demanded Fred.

"It's my French exchange dilemma, you fool!" said Jess.

"Thank God I've escaped from all that," said Fred. His French exchange partner, Joel, had managed to develop glandular fever, and wouldn't be coming. So Fred was going to be spared all this anguish.

"I have to fascinate the gorgeous Edouard, don't I?" Jess went on. "I've got to send him a photo of me, fast! And it's got to be digitally enhanced cos my real face is enough to make strangers vomit."

"You're right there," said Fred. "Even old friends like me can feel a little queasy—excuse me for a moment." He turned aside and pretended to throw up discreetly into his schoolbag.

"Cut it out and listen," said Jess. "So I'm coming over tonight, OK? I have to fascinate this French guy so I can marry him and live in Paris."

"I'm a tad disappointed," sighed Fred. "I'd assumed you would go for a rich American and live in L.A. Then I'd be able to masquerade as your pet hound and sleep in a fabulous gold kennel with en suite pavement. Dogs in L.A. really have what you could call a lifestyle."

"No chance," said Jess jokily. "Any dog of mine has got to be house-trained."

"Give me time!" begged Fred. "Practice makes perfect, you know. I'm sniffing lampposts already."

The bell went. Fred looked round anxiously and started to flap his lanky arms about.

"OK, OK," he said. "Come round my house at about eight

tonight. Not before. I'm on a 'homework before friends' regime after the poker game incident at Jack's last week."

Jess was relieved. She knew Fred was a genius when it came to computer graphics. She ran off to French. She was going to need all the French she could get. How deeply she regretted all those times she'd read *BLING!* magazine under the desk instead of listening to Mrs. Bailey explaining about those horrible French tenses. The present tense was the only one Jess could talk in. But since the concept of present tense captured her mood exactly, it was probably the only one she'd ever need.

At break she ambushed Flora by the tuck shop. Flora was buying some crisps, and when she saw Jess she looked guilty.

"Caught in the act!" said Jess.

Flora blushed. She was so cute. You could make Flora blush easily. And you could make tears come to her eyes by saying the word "kittens." She also laughed helplessly whenever Jess cracked a joke. Jess's jokes weren't always the best. In fact, sometimes they were downright lame, so this was very kind of Flora.

"No, it's all right," said Flora. "I can have these crisps now, because I'm only going to have a salad for lunch, and I haven't had any chocolate for sixteen days." Flora had a perfect figure anyway. Jess envied her *Baywatch* boobs (natural, not silicone) and blond hair, which shone divinely in the sun. Flora loved the sun, and it seemed to shine more brightly when she was about, as if it loved her back.

Jess preferred the moon. It had a sad, fat face. Jess was a

creature of the night. She just hoped Edouard was into bats and owls, too. They could sit at the bottom of her garden together, gazing at the stars . . . and his hand would find hers in the dark, and . . .

Jess chose a chicken fajita and a chocolate milk shake, which was allegedly low-fat.

"Come on!" said Jess, waving *BLING!* magazine. "You've got to help me choose a nose and some lips for my makeover tonight."

Warm spring sunshine (no doubt attracted by Flora) flooded down onto Ashcroft School, and Jess and Flora huddled up on a bench in a cozy corner of the science quad with *BLING!* magazine. They had their lunch and gave the celebs marks out of ten for sex appeal. Nobody scored higher than seven, though. It was always strangely comforting to spot a little bit of cellulite on a celebrity's thigh.

"I'm glad I haven't got a French boy coming," said Flora. "It's bad enough having a girl. My dad's so embarrassing. He's always shouting at us. I'm scared that he'll make Marie-Louise cry."

"You're scared of everything," said Jess, finishing her chocolate milk shake with a loud and obscene rattling suck.

"It's true," admitted Flora. "I *am* terrified of just about *everything*."

"What are you most scared of?" asked Jess.

"Well, the curtains in the sitting room at my granny's house freak me out because they look a bit sinister, as if someone's hiding behind them," said Flora with a shudder. "And you know I've always had a bit of a thing about bats."

Flora nervously smoothed her golden hair, holding it

close to her neck and looking anxiously about in case some random daylight high school bat swooped down and got entangled. "What else? Oh, I'm scared of prize givings now, because of when I fell flat on my face coming down from the stage at Speech Day two years ago. That was the worst day of my life."

"Tell me about it!" agreed Jess. "My mum fell downstairs in a department store once. It was in Maskell's—you know, going down to the deli department—and she tripped and grabbed me as she fell, and carried me down with her." Jess shut her eyes and shuddered at the memory of it. "We landed in a chaos of salami. About seventy people were all staring, hoping we'd died."

There was a brief silence while Jess and Flora burped thoughtfully and screwed up their paper napkins.

"I think you're ever so brave, having a French boy, though," said Flora. "So much could go wrong."

"What could go wrong?" said Jess. "The only problem I'm going to have is that I can totally *not* speak French. We'll have to communicate in sign language. But hey! Who cares? It'll be a laugh."

In a dark corner of the furthest recesses of her mind, however, she did feel a horrid little shiver of panic.

✳ 3 ✳

"I found a photo of you on my PC," said Fred. "From that school trip to Oxford."

"Oh no!" said Jess. "That was last year! I was so young. Practically a fetus. I had terrible hair as well. I've got some more recent ones on this CD."

"Well, just take a look at what I've done so far," said Fred, with a mysterious smile. "You'd pay a fortune for this kind of image enhancement in L.A., you know." And he clicked on an icon called "New Improved Jess."

A monster appeared. It had the eyes of a frog, the mouth of a shark, and the nose of an anteater.

"I was planning to give you the arse of a baboon," said Fred. "That would be the icing on the cake."

Jess was tempted to pull Fred's hair. It drooped down around his shoulders in sad wispy locks. She was always nagging him to have it cut. But on the other hand, it was very handy when punishment was due.

However, she decided not to rise to his bait. Instead, she leant closer to the screen and examined the image closely, then whistled.

"Wow!" she breathed softly. "Is that really, really me? I'm almost in love with myself."

"Don't fight it," said Fred. "It's the sensible choice. You should sue your orthodontist, though."

"Is it true sharks grow new teeth all the time?" asked Jess. "I wish we did. You'd save a fortune on tooth-whitening toothpaste."

"What is toothpaste?" asked Fred.

"Shut up, Parsons, you're a total hobo," said Jess affectionately. "Now come on! Let's take a look at Scarlett Johansson's lips."

They looked at about a hundred photos of Scarlett Johansson, Beyoncé, and Angelina Jolie.

"So which of them do you rate?" asked Jess. "Who would be your secret sex goddess?"

"I don't believe in sex gods and goddesses," said Fred. "I'm a confirmed bachelor. Girls are so vile. Boys, too— he added hastily." Fred often said "he added hastily." Sometimes he sounded like somebody from an old-fashioned novel.

They messed around for a while trying to transplant Scarlett's lips onto Jess's face, but it didn't work. But Fred did manage somehow to get rid of Jess's spots, plump up her lips, and add a manic sparkle to her eye. On the screen, anyway. They printed the image and scrutinized it critically.

"Hey!" said Jess. "It's not bad! I look almost human. It's plastic surgery without the bruising."

"I could always add a little light bruising, if you prefer," said Fred, brandishing a fist. "No extra charge."

"When Edouard and I are installed in our palatial flat in Paris, you can come round and digitally enhance the children," said Jess.

"No thanks!" said Fred. "Those Frenchmen are jealous as hell. He'd probably challenge me to a duel or something." Downstairs, the Parsons family clock started to strike the hour.

"Oh no! Look at the time!" said Jess, aware that her mum would be cooking up a monster sulk if she was too late on a school night. "Well, thanks, Fred! You're a genius!" Jess pulled his hair with just a teeny dash of sadism. Fred grabbed her arm and gave her just the hint of a Chinese burn. Then it was time to leave.

When she got home, her mum was up in her study, talking on the phone. Jess ran upstairs.

"All right, then," her mother was saying. "But I'm not very happy about it. Ring me tomorrow evening and tell me how it went . . . I know, I know. Take care. Bye, Mum!"

"Was that Granny?" asked Jess, as her mum rang off. "What weren't you very happy about?" Her mum looked thoughtfully at her own fingernails and frowned.

"Oh, nothing really," she said. "Look how dirty my fingernails are. I couldn't find my gardening gloves."

"Mum! Never mind all this fingernail stuff! It's just a diversion. What's going on with Granny?"

"Nothing," said her mum, getting up suddenly. "It's nothing, really. It's just one of her silly ideas."

"What silly idea?" said Jess.

"It's nothing," said her mum. "Really. Honestly."

"Why are you lying to me?" asked Jess. "What's with this Granny mystery?"

"There is no mystery," said Mum. "She's just got a new friend, that's all."

"What? A boyfriend?" shrieked Jess. "Brilliant! How old is he?"

"No, no, it's not like that," said Mum, looking trapped and irritated. "It's not a man at all. It's just a woman."

"Maybe Granny's been a closet lezzer all these years!" said Jess. "Wow! That would be so cool! To have a gay grandma!"

"Don't be so silly!" Mum snapped. Jess recognized the signs of a serious storm brewing. She would have to resist all further gay-granny jokes and contain her curiosity. Her mum could be very obstinate and very secretive at times. Even now she was walking out of the room and going downstairs. Jess followed.

"Let's have some toast!" she said.

"That's the first sensible thing you've said all day," said Mum.

"It's the first sensible thing I've said all year," said Jess. Her mum's mood could always be improved with toast. But after the toast, Mum started staring into the distance and heaved a sigh.

"I did mean to do the vacuuming," she said dolefully. "And we'd better start getting Edouard's room ready."

"Where's he going to sleep?" asked Jess, with a sudden horrid panic. "He's not going to share my room!"

"No, no, he'll sleep in the little spare room," said Mum. "We'll have to clear all the junk out of there, though. We can do a couple of trips to the recycling center."

"Yes, and we can make it really nice, can't we?" said Jess. "Oh no! There are flowers on the curtains! It's way too feminine! What sort of curtains do boys like?"

"I haven't the faintest idea," said Mum. "It sounds rather a sexist notion, to be honest."

Jess ignored her mother's comments and ran to the phone and dialed Fred's number.

"Fred!" she said. "What sort of curtains do boys like?"

"Curtains? What are curtains?" asked Fred.

Typical. Boys really were from another planet. What would it be like to have one in the house, right here in her face all the time, for a whole two weeks?

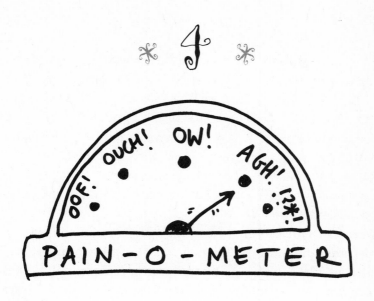

❋ 𝟺 ❋*

PAIN-O-METER

*J*ess went into her own room, which was at the back, on the ground floor. She liked it because it looked out onto the garden. There was a fabulous bedside light in the form of a screaming skull, and she'd hung a wonderful black sequined shawl on the wall. Her CDs were all arranged in alphabetical order (the one place where Jess had managed to be tidy) and her bald and charismatic teddy bear, Rasputin, reigned over the whole kingdom from his place on the pillow.

Jess had stuck up all her favorite posters. Eminem, mostly. Sometimes she thought Fred's eyes were rather like

Eminem's, only Fred was much more eccentric, with his long wispy hair and scarecrow arms.

Her letter to Edouard was ready on her desk. It had the proper stamp on and everything—for France. But it wasn't sealed up yet. She added the digitally enhanced photo and sealed the envelope. Then, seized by a strange impulse, she raised the envelope to her lips and planted just a tiny kiss on the back.

Oh no! There was a horrid lipstick smear! What a give-away! Hastily she opened the envelope, got a new one, and put the letter and the photo in. But the special stamp was still stuck to the old lipsticky envelope.

"Mum!" she shouted. "Have you got scissors? And glue?"

She heard Mum's footsteps coming downstairs. Jess quickly slipped the lipsticky envelope out of sight, down behind her desk, seconds before Mum burst in.

"Please can you knock before coming into my room? It really annoys me when you do that."

"And please can you *not* just yell when you want something?" Mum looked pretty irate, too. "I've told you time and time again, if you want something, come and find me and ask me politely."

"OK. Please may I have the scissors and the glue?"

"At this time of night? What for?"

"I'm making a birthday card for Michelle."

"Who's Michelle?" Who indeed? Jess had invented her—recklessly—a second ago.

"A girl at school. Her birthday's tomorrow and I totally forgot to get her a card today. Can you get me the scissors and glue?" Mum's eyes flared.

"Get them yourself! You know where they are! Up in my study, in the top right-hand drawer of my desk!"

"Yeah, but you just came downstairs! You could have brought them with you!"

"For God's sake, Jess! You're too idle to get out of your own way!"

Mum stomped off to the kitchen and began loading the dishwasher with unusual spite. Jess stomped upstairs as hard as she could, hoping to dislodge plaster from the ceiling below. She pulled out the drawer with such force that all the stuff inside went flying across the floor: scissors, glue, paper clips, drawing pins, pens, pencils, staples, Post-it notes . . .

She knelt down to pick them up, boiling with rage . . . and knelt down *on a drawing pin.* Luckily the pin was sideways, not with the sharp point upwards, so it was only four-star, not five-star, agony. Jess roared in pain. Mum wouldn't hear, though. She'd got the radio on downstairs, blaring out some news program.

I could die of drawing pins up here, thought Jess, *and she'd never know—she'd rather catch up with the latest terrorist outrages than protect her own daughter from harm in her own home.*

Jess threw everything violently back into the drawer and took the glue and scissors downstairs. She went into her bedroom and slammed the door. Now she had to retrieve the original envelope addressed to Edouard, so she could cut off the stamp. She heaved at her desk to move it away from the wall. At this moment there was a knock on her door.

"*What?*" roared Jess.

"I've put the kettle on. Would you like some hot chocolate?" called Mum through the door. A peace offering, evidently.

"No!" yelled Jess. "Wait—yes, please!" There was no need to prolong the row to the point of missing out on a chocolate fix. Jess stretched her arm behind the desk and scrabbled about for the envelope. As she got up again she hit her head on a high shelf.

"Ow! Owowowowow!" yelled Jess, rubbing her head. Was there any part of her body left to hurt? With a shrug, she cut the special stamp off the lipsticky envelope and stuck it on the new envelope with glue. Then she screwed the lipsticky envelope up violently and threw it at the bin. It missed. No, wait! She had to copy Edouard's address.

Jess retrieved the screwed-up lipsticky envelope, smoothed it out, and copied Edouard's name and address onto the new envelope. Her head still hurt from the shelf, and her knee still hurt from the drawing pin.

"I hope you're worth all this hassle, you stinkin' frog!" she growled to the address. Already Edouard had caused her major injury and a nasty little row between her and Mum. Although, to be honest, they were perfectly capable of whipping up a row between them without any help from anyone else. Jess wondered how it would have been if Dad had stayed part of the family. Much better, probably. She sighed.

Her mum knocked at the door. Jess threw the crumpled-up lipsticky envelope into the bin, then called, "Come in!" It sounded stupidly formal. Her mum entered carrying a big mug of chocolate and a ginger biscuit on a plate.

"Lovely, thanks, Mum," said Jess. "Sorry I was grumpy."

"Sorry I was," said Mum, and foolishly hugged Jess without putting down the hot chocolate first. Some of it slopped out and landed on Jess's arm.

"Ow!" shrieked Jess. "Ow! You've burnt me now!"

"Sorry, sorry!" said Mum, hastily putting down the mug. Some more of it slopped out right onto the letter to Edouard—the new, clean envelope!

"Oh my God!" cried Jess, whipping a tissue out of the box and mopping the chocolate off the letter and her arm. "Everything's going wrong! Just everything!"

"It's only a little bit on the corner," said Mum guiltily. "Anyway, French people love chocolate."

"I'm not sure they love it on their actual letters," snarled Jess. "Why is absolutely everything going wrong today?"

"Mercury's retrograde," said Mum darkly. Like most old hippies, she was seriously into astrology. "The car wouldn't start this morning."

"The car wouldn't start because it's a heap," said Jess.

"Never mind that," said Mum. "Show me your card."

"What card?"

"The card you were making for Michelle."

"I've decided to leave it to the morning," said Jess. "I'm too tired. My brain's asleep already. I don't like Michelle much anyway. I might just not bother."

"Oh no. Do make her one in the morning," said Mum. "You won't regret it. I think her mother comes into the library." Mum kissed Jess and went out. Jess smiled to herself. Michelle was a fiction, a complete invention, a person who simply did not exist. Yet Mum already imagined she knew Michelle's mum by sight.

Please God, Jess prayed, *let Mum not be too eccentric while Edouard's here.*

After she'd finished the hot chocolate, she took the mug out to the kitchen, where her mother was wiping down the worktops and still listening to the news. Jess put the dirty mug in the dishwasher. Her mum watched in amazement.

"What's this?" she asked. "Why aren't you just shoving your dirty mugs under your bed as usual?"

"I'll ignore that remark," said Jess. "We've got to keep the house clean and tidy while Edouard's here. I'm starting the new regime now. And will you please get rid of all those spiders' webs, Mum."

"You know I like spiders," said Mum. "They catch flies. Flies are really revolting. You wouldn't tolerate a visitor who pooed in the sugar bowl, would you?"

"Never say anything like that again!" said Jess. For a split second she hadn't been able to stop herself thinking about Edouard as the visitor who . . . The image would haunt her all her life. "Anyway," Jess went on, "please get rid of those webs! It looks like the Addams family home up on the landing."

"All right, all right!" said Mum. "Stop nagging. And if you want the place spotless for when Edouard comes, you'll have to lend a hand."

"Of course!" said Jess. "You do the spiders, though. You know I've got a thing about them."

Suddenly the phone rang. Mum frowned and looked at her watch. She hated people ringing after ten o'clock. Jess immediately felt guilty, even though it was only ten past. Maybe it was Flora or Fred. She grabbed it.

"Hello?" she said.

"Hello, you fabulous creature! This is your ancient dad!"

"Dad!" Jess almost whooped with joy. "It's Dad!" she said to Mum.

"I had worked that one out," said Mum rather sarcastically, and went out of the kitchen looking as if she had something important to do.

"Mum sends her love," said Jess.

"Give her mine, give her mine," said Dad, sounding a bit nervous. Her parents were such retards. OK, they were divorced, but they still acted strange around each other.

Jodie's parents were divorced, but they actually all went on holidays together, even though Jodie's dad had a new wife and a baby and everything. Jess wished her parents could be a bit more relaxed.

"So how are things in gorgeous St. Ives?" asked Jess. "I'm so jealous! I wish I was there. I want to hear the seagulls! Hold the phone out of the window."

"It's dark, dumbo!" said Dad. "The seagulls are all asleep."

"Don't call me dumbo," said Jess. "It's a bit too close to jumbo."

"I refuse to discuss diets, weight, or whether your arse looks big at the moment," said Dad. "Thank God I can't see you. All I can say is, you sound beautifully slim."

"That's only cos I'm holding my voice in," said Jess. "But does my arse sound big?"

"I'll ignore that!" said her dad, laughing. "I rang up for a civilized conversation about the arts, and all I get is obscenity."

Out in the hall, Jess's mum started up the vacuum cleaner. How typical. It was as if she wanted to blot him out.

"What's that noise?" asked Dad. "It sounds as if a flying saucer's landed."

"It's only Mum vacuuming," said Jess. "Hang on, I'll close the kitchen door."

She put the phone down on the table and shut out most of the noise. It was so great talking to Dad again. If only Mum could join in.

"Are you still there?" said Jess, picking up. There was silence. "Dad?" she said, puzzled. "Dad? . . . *Dad?*"

"Only joking," said Dad. "I was playing hide-and-seek. It's much easier by phone."

"I could hear your strange snorting breath," said Jess. "I thought you'd fainted or something."

"No, no," said Dad. "I'll be fainting soon, though, with all the stress."

"Yeah, right! The stress of your amazingly relaxed life by the sea. I've got to come and visit! I'm so jealous! I haven't even seen your new house down there yet."

"Well, I've got a plan," said Dad. "Listen. I'm having an exhibition soon. It opens on the seventeenth. I'll send you an invite with all the details. I just had this brilliant idea. Why don't you come down here for the private view? It's on the Saturday night, at six o'clock. Mum could put you on the train on Saturday morning. I could meet the train. You could spend Saturday night here, then we could have Sunday lunch in a lovely restaurant overlooking the harbor, then I could put you on the afternoon train home."

"Oh my God!" cried Jess. "That is totally fabulous! I'll go and ask Mum now!"

"No, wait!" said Dad. "Don't ask her now. Not if she's vacuuming. Vacuuming is bad news. It means she's moments from meltdown. Wait for the right moment."

"Why don't you ask her yourself?" said Jess.

"No, no! I can't sweet-talk her like you can!" Dad had stopped sounding relaxed and jokey. "The thing is—I always sound like a—well, a complete prat whenever I ask her for a favor. You can, you know—get round her with bunches of flowers, er . . . unexpected bouts of washing-up, you know the sort of thing."

"Don't worry," said Jess. "I'll get it sorted. I can't wait. I'll actually see your house and everything! Brilliant! Brilliant!"

"Well, I think you're old enough to travel down on your own, now," said Dad. "After all, you're nearly—what is it? Thirty-five?"

"I've been old enough to travel on my own for years," said Jess drily.

"I know, I know," said Dad, getting back into jokey mode but still sounding a bit flustered. "You've always been a lot older than me, even when you were a baby."

"Yes," said Jess. "I'm an Old Soul. I know. You told me that once before. It was an attempt to make me stop singing in the car. You also said I had a voice like a crow. You old sweet-talker."

"Crows are a favorite, though," said Dad. "Although ravens are more majestic. And rooks are . . ."

"Spare me the ornithology!" yelled Jess, laughing. "I'm still not interested."

"OK. I've got to go now," said Dad. "I'd forgotten how late it was. I know what Mum's like about people who ring after ten. Oh God! I hope I haven't blown it. I shall have to go and have a lie down."

"Bye then, Dad! I'll ring you as soon as I've fixed it all up."

"Right! Good girl. Give my love to Mum—and have some yourself, you gorgeous creature."

"Bye, Dad! Love you!"

Jess slammed down the receiver joyously and ran upstairs. Mum was on the landing, wearing a fixed frown and vacuuming the ceiling. Jess just knew it would be a bad time to ask. Her dad was so right. But she couldn't help herself.

"Mum!" said Jess. "Switch it off for a minute!"

"Just now you were nagging me to do it!" shouted Mum. "There's still some webs in the corners."

"Never mind that now!" shouted Jess. "Let me tell you what Dad said."

"In a minute!" shouted her mum. "I've nearly finished."

Jess waited. The excitement inside her curdled slightly. Making her wait was her mum's way of getting back at her dad. Jess had never properly understood why they had separated, all those years ago. She'd only been a baby. Deep inside her most secret heart, she was terrified that one day she'd find out that they split up because of her.

Mum switched off the vacuum cleaner. The engine sound died in an echoey way in the stairwell. Jess's confidence wilted also. Maybe she really should wait for a better moment.

"Dad sends his love," she said. "I told him you sent yours."

"OK," said Mum. She looked sulky, though.

Jess made a huge effort to recapture the excitement of her dad's wonderful invite.

"Listen, Mum!" she said. "It's brilliant! Dad's invited me down for his private view! He says if you put me on the train, he'll meet it and I can stay Saturday night and come back on Sunday. It'll be brilliant! Oh please! I haven't seen his house yet and I'm dying to go down there!"

"What about your homework?" asked her mum, looking suspicious.

"I'll do it on the train! I'll have hours and hours. I promise."

"When is this?" demanded her mum edgily.

"Er, he said soon. The seventeenth, I think he said."

Mum's face sort of collapsed into exasperation. But it was a kind of satisfied exasperation. Almost as if she'd been waiting for an excuse.

"Typical!" she said. "That's the weekend when the French boy will be here! It's impossible. Just typical of your father. I sent him an e-mail telling him we had this exchange student coming. In fact, I asked him if he could come up here for the weekend and help to entertain Edouard. I don't suppose he mentioned that."

"No," said Jess. She felt desolate, crushed, defeated. The wonderful plan of going to see Dad seemed to wither and writhe away into ashes, like a poem written on a burning piece of paper. A huge ball of tears welled up inside her. She felt like screaming. Why was her life such utter crap?

"I'm going to bed, then," she snapped. She didn't even kiss Mum goodnight: she stormed back downstairs to her room and slammed the door.

Once she was in bed, and the worst of her rage had subsided, she started to fantasize that she had better parents. If only she could do a swap. Madonna and Brad Pitt, maybe. Or Samantha Jones from *Sex and the City*. Without the sex, obviously. And . . . um . . . Frasier? Eventually Jess drifted into an uneasy sleep, and dreamed her dad was the prime minister.

Next morning breakfast was a bit tense, but neither Jess nor her mum mentioned the night before. The radio did most of the talking. Jess kissed Mum goodbye before she left for school, and Mum sort of clutched pathetically at her sleeve.

"Love you, despite my awfulness," said Mum gruffly.

"I love you despite your awfulness, too," said Jess. It was an awkward truce, as usual. If only Dad had realized the date of his exhibition clashed with Edouard's visit. If only they'd talk to each other properly instead of this constant *ask Mum tell Dad* business.

Jess sighed. She had to sort her parents out, get them to be proper friends, shape up and stop being such losers. She also had to find out what was happening with Granny. But first, looming large on the horizon but as yet without a face or identity, she had to confront the enormous, exciting enigma of Edouard.

A few days later, the letters and photos started to arrive from the French exchange students. First to arrive was Jodie's. Jodie was one of Jess's best mates, although not quite so close as Flora. She was shortish and darkish and had terrible spots. She was always ready for a laugh and was so full of energy and enthusiasm, it made Jess feel tired. When she was in a strop, Jodie could be ferocious. But most of the time she was nice, if a little pushy.

"Guess what!" said Jodie, bursting into the classroom before morning registration. "I've had a letter from Gerard, and here's his photo!" Everybody crowded round.

It was a really small photo, the sort you get in passport booths. Gerard wasn't smiling. His hair was dark and slicked back. His lips were thin and he was wearing rimless glasses. His ears stuck out a bit. The light in the photo booth hadn't been very good and there was something just a teensy bit sinister about the image.

"He's obviously going to be a pedophile when he grows up," said Fred.

"Shut up, Fred!" said Jess, punching Fred in the ribs. "He's lovely. He looks gorgeous. He's a bit like what's-his-name Fiennes." Secretly, though, she had to agree—Gerard did look weird.

"His dad's a patissier," said Jodie. "He makes pastries and stuff. I'm going to pig out when I go over there."

"So am I," said Jess. "I'll be gorging for England! Croissant overdose!"

Just then Flora arrived with a photo of her exchange partner, Marie-Louise. Everyone crowded round again. Marie-Louise was kind of cute but homely-looking, with short curly black hair and a nerdy smile.

"Three out of ten for sex appeal," said Whizzer in his usual gross, sex-obsessed way.

"Well, you wouldn't even get one out of ten," said Jess. "Your exchange partner will probably need psychotherapy."

Jess was really annoyed that Edouard hadn't bothered to send a letter and a photo yet. She hated him already.

But the next day, Edouard's letter did arrive. It was waiting for her on the doormat when she got home. Jess ripped it open right there in the hall, with trembling hands and a thudding heart. What if he was hideous? What if he was vile? The tiny photo fell facedown onto the hall floor. She snatched it up, prepared for the worst.

My God! He was adorable! Edouard had thick dark hair, big brown eyes, and lovely pouty lips. His nose was straight and his ears were tastefully close to his head, not sticking out like Gerard's. Jess decided she didn't hate him after all.

She unfolded the letter. It was written on paper covered with small blue squares. Edouard's handwriting was strange and loopy, and he did his "R"s in a weird old-fashioned way.

Hello Jess, it went. I present myself at you I am the French exchange partenaire. I am call Edouard Fenix and I lives in Chignon-sur-Forgue. My father is architect and my mother teach on the elementary school. I haves one brother Alain he has 19 years and one sister Alice she have 10 years. Our house is in the river. We have dogs two lovelys Hector et Joubert. I am looking forwards to my visit in your house. I likes the sailing, chess, and ento-mologie. My subject favorite is the mathematique. After school I will go on the engineering college. I like England and Manchester United is my loved football team. Please say your mother I am allergic to gooseberries. Please write me all on the subject of yourself, and send foto, Good kisses, Edouard.

"Send photo," eh? Obviously Jess's digitally enhanced image hadn't arrived yet. "Good kisses"! How forward! But what a sweet letter. Particularly that bit about their house being in the river. It seemed as if Edouard was going to bring them plenty of laughs. She just hoped he didn't say anything obscene, by accident. Or rather, she hoped he *did*.

"Mum!" she said. "There's a letter from Edouard!"

Mum was kneeling on the kitchen floor, cleaning the oven in honor of Edouard's looming visit. If Edouard ever opened the oven, he would certainly be impressed. Actually, the spare room they were getting ready for him was so small, there would almost be more room in the oven.

"Oooh, let me see!" said Mum, getting up and washing her hands.

"He's sent a photo," said Jess, holding it out for her mum to see. "He reminds me of somebody, but I can't think who it is."

"A young Colin Firth, apart from the lips," said Mum, without a moment's hesitation. If only she'd had the fore-sight to go and live in Hollywood, she could have become a glamorous casting director instead of a nerdy librarian. "You know, Mark Darcy in the Bridget Jones films."

"Yes," said Jess. "I suppose Edouard could be Colin Firth's long-lost love-child. Although he does say his dad's an architect."

"An architect? Oh good!" said Mum. She was a bit of a snob sometimes. "May I read it?"

Mum was being extra-polite since the row the other night. She took the letter and, to Jess's amazement, sniffed it.

"Stop, Mum!" yelled Jess. "Gross! Don't sniff it! What are you expecting, for God's sake? Scent or something?"

"No, it's just . . . I love the smell of French paper," said Mum. She was sometimes so weird.

"He says he's allergic to gooseberries," said Jess. Her

mum didn't answer. Her eyes flashed down through the lines. Being a librarian, she could read at lightning speed.

"It's a shame about the gooseberries," she smiled, folding up the letter and giving it back. "I was planning to include them in every meal. Bacon, egg, and gooseberries for breakfast . . ."

"Tomato and gooseberry sandwiches for lunch!" added Jess.

"Gooseberry pizza . . . oh well, never mind. He sounds very nice."

"What's all that *good kisses* rubbish?" said Jess, blushing.

"Oh, the French all say that to each other all the time," said Mum. "*Bons baisers.* It's what you write at the end of a letter. It doesn't matter whether you're writing to your crazy aunt, your aged grandpa, or your English exchange partner."

Jess felt deeply disappointed, but tried to hide it. She wondered what Edouard would say if—or when—he was really mad about her, and how long it would take to get him there.

It was going to be quite tricky getting up close and personal with Edouard. At school her mates would all be around. And at home Mum would constantly be hovering, playing—er—gooseberry.

Suddenly a brilliant, brilliant idea shot across Jess's mind. She almost choked with excitement. But before she could take it any further, she had to make a phone call to her dad. A confidential one.

Budget face-lift?

THIS WAY UP

"I'm just going outside to deadhead the daffodils," said Mum. "It'll be dark soon."

Brilliant! A perfect window of opportunity! It was almost as if God was on her side. "Thanks, Old Boy," she whispered to the Divine One, and waited and watched till her mum went out. Then she raced upstairs and grabbed the study phone.

"Dad!" she yelled, the moment he picked up. "You know I thought I wouldn't be able to make it down to your exhibition because of the French boy?"

"Don't tell me!" said Dad. "He's been slightly run over.

I've been to the witch doctor but I wasn't expecting it to have worked so soon."

"No, no," laughed Jess. "Listen! I haven't got much time, because Mum's out deadheading the daffodils and I don't know how many there are!"

"Believe me," said Dad drily, "there will be hundreds."

"Well, listen up!" said Jess. "How about this idea? I come down to your private view, but I bring Edouard with me!" There was a brief and rather horrid pause.

"Er—would I have to talk to him?" asked Dad. "In French? I'm not at my best with foreigners."

"You won't have to say a word!" promised Jess. "I'll do all the talking. He can speak English anyway. I've had a letter from him, and it was all in English. There won't be a problem."

"Uh—where could he sleep?" pondered Dad, the driveling fool.

"The sofa!" yelled Jess. "You must have a sofa! He can sleep under the kitchen table! Anywhere!"

There was another silence, this time even longer, punctuated only by strange *um*s and *ahh*s.

"Oh, come on, Dad!" begged Jess. "Just say yes! This means so much to me. I can't bear the thought of missing your exhibition. And I'll be so proud of you, with Edouard there."

In Jess's imagination, she and Edouard mingled attractively with a throng of elegant people sipping champagne, while her dad, with slightly more hair than usual and better teeth, was interviewed for a TV arts program by a charismatic woman in black leather. Edouard stared down at her and whispered, "Your fazzair is so vairy talented. But zen, so are you, Jess . . . darlingue." And because the room was packed with celebs, they were forced so close together that his breath almost melted her mascara.

"OK," said Dad. "But you'll have to run it past Hitler." This was clearly a reference to Mum. Jess heard the back door open downstairs.

"Great!" she whispered. "Hitler's just come in from his deadheading. I'll ask him now."

"Good luck," said Dad. "You're going to need it," he added ominously.

"Rubbish!" said Jess. "Order an extra ton of canapés for the private view, cos we'll be there!"

She rang off and raced downstairs. This was such a brilliant idea! She would have hours and hours of private time with Edouard! They could wander around the quaint streets of St. Ives, hand in hand. Or sit on the beach, staring at the surf, with their arms round each other. And there would be that long train journey down, hours and hours of it. And the long journey back again . . . They could stare into each other's eyes all the way. Jess's eyes watered in anticipation.

"Mum!" she said. "You know Edouard's visit coincides with Dad's exhibition? Well, I've thought of a brilliant idea. Edouard could go down there with me! Dad says it's fine by him. Edouard can sleep on his sofa. And Edouard will be company for me on the train, and everything—it'll be safer if I've got somebody to travel with, won't it?"

Jess waited for her mum's response. She felt poised between a glorious world full of golden light, and a black abyss. It was possibly a bit like what happened after you died, with Mum playing God. Mum's eyes flashed, and for a split second Jess almost heard the distant rumble of an angry thunderbolt getting warmed up.

"No!" The thunderbolt whizzed past her right ear, slightly scorching her hair. "It's out of the question! It's a ridiculous idea!"

"But you said you wanted Dad to take some responsibility—help out with Edouard!"

"No! Stop it, Jess! It just won't wash! Who's going to pay for his train ticket, for a start? Have you any idea what it costs, going all the way down to St. Ives by train?"

"I'll pay for it!" said Jess. "I'll use my savings money."

"No, you will not!" said Mum, flames blazing from her nostrils. "I have to countersign for that account, so you can forget it. What? Fritter away your precious savings on a crazy wild-goose chase like this? Edouard won't want to go anyway. He won't want to be separated from his French friends. He'll want to spend some time with them over the weekend. They'll probably have things organized for them."

Jess's heart sank. She felt herself slipping into the black abyss.

"But Dad was so much looking forward to meeting Edouard," she said lamely.

"If he's so keen on meeting him, tell him to come up to town and take us all out to dinner or something," said Mum. "Now, that *would* be helpful."

"But Dad was so looking forward to seeing me!" whined Jess.

"He knows our address," said Mum with horrid, crisp sarcasm. "I'm going to have a bath." She went upstairs. Jess's wonderful fantasy was over. Her heart was full of cinders.

She rang her dad, from the kitchen this time, so as not to be overheard by her mum in the bath.

"Dad!" she said quietly. "I'm gutted. Mum says it's out of the question."

"Hmmm," said Dad. "I thought so." He didn't sound quite as devastated as Jess had hoped. "Sorry, old bean."

"She says if you really want to help, come up to town and take us all out."

"Much as I'd love to do that, of course," said Dad hastily, as if he'd worked it out beforehand, "because the exhibition's on for the whole fortnight of Edouard's visit, it's impossible . . . I have to be there, you see, all the time. It's only a tiny little gallery."

Dad's glorious champagne-filled private view shriveled, in Jess's imagination, into a tiny feast in a shoe box involving three dormice and an acorn or two. She was too disappointed even to speak. There was a deep, dismal silence.

"Cheer up," said Dad. "Talking to foreigners isn't my strong point."

"That sounds more like a reason for you to be cheerful, not me," said Jess acidly. "OK, then, Dad. Love you. I'll call again soon."

She hung up before her dad even had time to reply. He could be so kind of deliberately, conveniently weak sometimes. Jess heaved such a huge sigh, she seemed to dislocate one of her ribs. After such a traumatic event, there was really only one thing that could cheer her up. She'd just have to pin Edouard's photo up on her noticeboard and gaze at it all evening, while pigging out on Doritos and dips.

Next day there was a more gratifying scenario. She took the photo to school. A crowd gathered. Loads and loads of French exchange partners had now sent photos. Tom's looked like a trout. Alice's looked like a sniper. Henry's looked like a gangster.

"OK, here's Edooooo-argh!" announced Jess, holding up the photo.

"Oh, he's a babe!"

"He's adorable!"

'He's gorgeous!"

The girls would be all over him, then, the bitches. Jess made rapid plans never to let her friends anywhere near him.

Then Jess sensed Fred standing behind her.

"What do you think, Parsons?" she asked, turning round. Fred grinned.

"Now that's what I call a sex god," said Fred. "Has he received your photo yet? One can almost hear the sardonic French laughter. How are you going to deal with it? A paper bag over your head? A Halloween mask? I think I have an old one in my garage. You're welcome to borrow it if you think it'll help."

Jess pulled Fred's hair extremely hard, and he pinched her earlobes with vicious panache. It was horrid of Fred to tease her on this most sensitive of subjects. He must know how terrified she was at the thought of Edouard looking at the photo of her, let alone her real, horrid pasty face.

A couple of days later, there was another letter from Edouard. Or rather, it was a postcard, but contained in an envelope. The postcard was a picture of a French town hall, lit up at night. Dullsville, clearly. But Jess didn't waste any time looking at the picture.

Dear Jess, I have receive you letter with photo, it said in Edouard's cute loopy writing. *You are very pritty. I am waiting to see you in England. I am counting the day. My mother send the respects to yours mother. See you on 21st, your friend Edouard. Bons Baisers. x*

A kiss! A kiss! He'd put a shy little "x" at the bottom of the card! And he'd said she was very pritty! He was clearly smitten! There was no sardonic French laughter at her hideousness, only a kiss! Oh my God!

Jess was somehow thrilled to bits, and yet, at the same time, scared as hell. What was going to happen when they met face to face? When Edouard saw her real face, not the digitally enhanced image? Oh well. She would soon find out.

douard was due to arrive, rather excitingly, at midnight. Apparently it was an enormously long drive from France—hours and hours and hours. They would be shattered. All the English host families turned up in their cars, parked in the pitch-black school yard, and waited. It was almost sinister.

"It's insane," grumbled Mum. "They'll be totally exhausted. Why on earth couldn't they come by plane?"

"Well, don't hassle me about it!" said Jess. "Talk to Mrs. Bailey. I'm sure she'll be only too happy to explain."

But where was Mrs. Bailey? Where, indeed, was anybody? it was too dark to see, with only the headlights of cars occasionally silhouetting clumps of people talking.

"I'm getting out," said Jess. "I'm going to look for Flora."

Now the moment of truth had arrived, Jess felt sick with anxiety. But on the other hand, the thought of meeting Edouard in person made her heart race. He had said she was "pritty" and sent her a kiss! Jess had brought his postcard. It was in her pocket. By now it was very worn and dog-eared, but having it with her gave Jess a little bit of courage. It was proof that Edouard liked the way she looked. And after all, he was, according to his photo, one of the fittest among the whole French gang.

Flora loomed out of the dark and grabbed Jess's arm. Jess was glad it was dark. Once Edouard saw Flora in daylight, he would certainly lose interest in Jess.

"God! I'm so scared!" said Flora. "What if I don't get on with her?"

"Of course you'll get on with her," said Jess. Marie-Louise looked sweet and friendly, and she had the tact not to be fabulously sexy—what more could you want in a houseguest?

Suddenly a large set of headlights swung in off the main road. The coach! Here it was! Flora and Jess clung to each other in excitement and dread.

"Oh my God!" said Jess. "It's the Norman Invasion all over again!"

They had done the Battle of Hastings in history and rooted for the English king, who was called (strangely) Harold Godwin. But Harold had received an arrow in his eye and William the Conqueror had conquered, big-time.

"Perhaps you'll be conquered by Edouard," said Flora. "He will enslave you. I can see it all."

"I will not!" retorted Jess. "If anything, he's going to be my slave. Watch this space."

The bus rolled up, stopped, and then did a stupid turning and reversing maneuver that seemed totally unnecessary. It only prolonged the agony and filled the whole area with carbon monoxide. Pale smudgy faces looked out of the bus's dark windows, but it was impossible to see any details. It was impossible even to see what sex they were.

Eventually the bus driver parked, turned off the engine, and opened the door. A French English teacher appeared. She seemed to be a woman, although it wasn't totally certain, what with the darkness, her nerdy anorak, and her woolly hat. She climbed down and greeted Mrs. Bailey, the English French teacher. They shook hands and kissed each other several times on each cheek. It took forever. The French English teacher spoke in English to show off, and the English French teacher spoke in French to demonstrate that she, too, was one hell of a linguist. Everybody else just waited, wilted, and yawned.

"Right!" Mrs. Bailey climbed up the bus steps and called for attention. "As the French party get off the bus, I'll call out the name of the English host. When you hear your name, please come forward and welcome your guest."

A rather cute but tubby French boy was the first to appear. The French and English teachers coordinated their lists. "George Simpson!" called Mrs. Bailey.

"Simpson's is a lardass, then," whispered Jess. "But I quite like him nonetheless."

"Yes," said Flora. "Cuddly. Something for the winter months, probably."

A small blond girl appeared, wrapped in a terrible pale pink padded jacket.

"*Nul points* for the clothes," said Jess. "She looks like a prawn." Flora started laughing hysterically.

"It's going to take all night!" she said. "I'm asleep already."

"We're all asleep," said Jess. "This is just a terrible nightmare." *Come on, come on, Edouard,* she thought.

"Er—Justine Barraclough!" called Mrs. Bailey. Justine fought her way through the crowd and took possession of the human prawn. A tall dark handsome boy appeared.

"I bet that's Edouard!" hissed Flora. "He's gorgeous!"

Jess's heart started to race, and she got ready to claim her Prince Charming.

"Jodie Gordon!" called Mrs. Bailey. Oh no! It wasn't Edouard—it was Gerard! Gerard whose photo had looked a bit weird, with sticking-out ears and thin pedophile lips!

"How amazing!" whispered Flora. "He's nothing like his photo!"

"He should definitely sack his PR department!" said Jess. "That photo did him absolutely no favors. He's such a babe!"

Jodie barged forward and grabbed the gorgeous Gerard. He grinned and kissed her on both cheeks. Wow! Jess felt a thrill of excitement. That was what Edouard was going to do to her, any minute now, when it was his turn.

Several other kids got off, and the crowd started to thin. Once an English host family had claimed their guest, of course, they drove off home to a hot chocolate and bed. A short dark girl appeared, blinking in the swirling headlights of departing cars.

"I think that's Marie-Louise!" said Flora. The teachers consulted their lists. Mrs. Bailey looked up.

"Flora Barclay!" she called.

"Bingo!" said Jess. Flora left her side and went forward. Jess watched as Marie-Louise kissed Flora on both cheeks, smiled, and started talking straightaway. She hoped Edouard would be confident like that. She waited. Her mum joined her.

"With any luck," murmured Mum, "they'll have left him behind at a service station."

There was hardly anybody left now. Jess began to panic. How embarrassing to be the last! And nobody would be able to see the magnificent Edouard and envy her. A small, scruffy, nerdy boy appeared in the bus doorway, wearing glasses. A kind of young French version of Harry Potter only without the magical charisma. *He must be the bus driver's kid or something—come along for the ride,* thought Jess with a grin.

"Jess Jordan!" called Mrs. Bailey.

"No!" breathed Jess. "It can't be! He's just a kid." She didn't move. Her mum pushed her forward.

"Go on!" she whispered. "Go and get him! The poor little thing looks shattered."

Jess stumbled forward, as if in a dream. The French teacher placed a friendly hand on her arm and steered her towards the small boy. He'd climbed down the steps now, and he hardly came up to Jess's nose. Oh my God! Forget Harry Potter! He was a Hobbit.

And what's with the glasses? she thought. It was sort of cheating to take your glasses off for a photo. Though Jess's mum did it all the time. In Mum's case it was a pathetic attempt to appear young and trendy. In Edouard's case it was treachery.

"Jess!" said Mrs. Bailey. "This is Edouard, your French partner."

"Hello!" said Jess. Edouard held out his hand in an awkward, formal kind of way.

"Hello!" he said. His voice was kind of squeaky. *My God,* thought Jess. *He's a child, a mere child. I can forget all thoughts of flirting. Babysitting would be more appropriate.*

At this point Jess's mum came forward, shook Edouard warmly by the hand, and led him away to the car, talking away nineteen to the dozen in fluent French. Jess had been dreading the thought of her mum showing off her language skills, but as it had turned out, it had saved the day.

Jess followed them to the car, her heart sinking. Edouard was so small he could hardly carry his bag. Oh well. They'd been worried about the limited space available in the spare room. They needn't have worried. You could have accommodated a whole flock of little Edouards in there, like a kind of burrow full of meerkats.

Jess was already dreading taking him into school tomorrow. Especially as everybody had seen his photo and was expecting a love god. Oh God! What if somebody actually laughed out loud? Jess made urgent plans to call in sick for the next fortnight.

*O*nce Jess got in the car, another major problem
instantly became clear. There was a really terrible stink.

"Don't mention the whiff," said Mum, starting up the car.

"Don't just talk like that in front of him!" said Jess, embarrassed.

"Don't worry," said Mum. "His command of our native
tongue is tentative to the point of nonexistent."

"Why are you talking in that weird way, like somebody
out of a costume drama?"

"Merely," said Mum, "to guard against the eventuality

of our guest's comprehension of certain little giveaway phrases."

"Well, at least use language that *I* can understand!" said Jess.

"Don't raise your voice to me," murmured Mum, turning out of the school drive and heading for home. "He'll be very sensitive to tones of voice. Especially angry ones. And the poor little thing is totally shattered."

"We should have a code name for him," said Jess. "How about 'the Queen'?"

"Nice idea," said Mum. "Now try to be nice to the Queen. She's had a terrible journey. At least look over your shoulder and smile at her."

Jess looked over her shoulder and smiled encouragingly at Edouard. He looked at her and gave a kind of deranged nod.

"We'll soon be home!" said Jess. Edouard frowned and looked panicky. Surely he understood four words? One of which was "be'? Jess sighed—but tried to hide it. "Soon be home!" she repeated, trying for a soothing tone of voice. "Only ten minutes!" Edouard shrugged and looked as if he was going to cry. Jess forced a huge smile out of her emergency smile store and turned back.

"The Queen didn't understand a word of that," she reported. "I think she's on the edge of a nervous breakdown."

"I've already told her it's only ten minutes to the house," said Mum. "In French."

"Don't use the F-word!" said Jess. "Or the Queen will know we're talking about her!"

"OK, then," said Mum. "Urdu."

"What?"

"Urdu—it's an Indian language."

"I don't like the sound of it," said Jess. "Sounds a bit like doo-doo."

"I told you not to mention the whiff," said Mum.

"I've been trying to ignore it," said Jess. "But I can't help feeling majorly pissed off that the Queen is not only barely visible to the naked eye, but also smells of dog poo."

"For goodness' sake, Jess," said Mum, in a relaxed, pleasant tone of voice that belied her vicious message, "if you don't stop whingeing and start being pleasant about the poor little Queen, you won't get any pocket money from now till Christmas."

Nobody talked for the rest of the journey. Mum put a South African gospel CD on to try and create a soothing atmosphere. They arrived, parked the car, and went indoors. Soon they were standing awkwardly in the kitchen, blinking in the harsh fluorescent light.

"I must get this light changed," said Mum. "It doesn't do anybody any favors." Edouard's eyes were red and his face was so pale, it was almost green.

In theory he was now able to see that Jess was not quite as "pritty" as in the digitally enhanced photo she had sent. However, he appeared to be avoiding looking at her. Jess didn't care, obviously. So she had deceived him a bit by getting Fred to blot out a few spots and put a sparkle in her eye? Edouard had actually concealed the fact that he was a speccy nerd, smaller than the average teddy bear, and stank like a dogs' lavatory.

Mum got some bread out of the bread bin and flourished it, saying something in French, and Edouard answered, apparently in the negative.

"Go and show Edouard up to his room, please, Jess," said Mum. Her voice sounded unreal. It was like bad acting.

"No, you," said Jess. She couldn't bear to be on her own with him for a split second. Not tonight.

"Let's all go, then," said Mum. They trooped upstairs. Mum showed Edouard where the bathroom was—in French—and offered him the opportunity to take a bath, which he also declined. He clearly just wanted to be shut away in his own little burrow and cry himself to sleep.

"Good night!" said Jess with enthusiasm, waving absurdly as she turned away. The smile was damned hard work.

"Goo'night!" replied Edouard, but without a smile. It was awful, just awful.

Jess and Mum regrouped in the kitchen. Even the kitchen looked wrong and strange: it had been cleaned and tidied in honor of Edouard's arrival. It looked uncomfortable, like somebody else's place.

"Let's have a hot chocolate!" said Jess.

"I'm worried about him," said Mum, as she put the kettle on. "What a terrible journey for the poor little thing."

"If you call him a poor little thing one more time," said Jess, "I am going to be sick all over your nice clean floor. He's fifteen, Mum!"

"All the same," said Mum. "He brings out the mother hen in me."

"A shame I never managed that particular conjuring trick," said Jess acidly. She cut herself a huge doorstop of bread. It seemed ludicrous, but Jess was beginning to feel jealous of Edouard. It was as if her mum loved him more than she loved Jess. Though this feeling was plainly insane, it caused a heartache that could only be soothed by a huge cheese sandwich and a hot chocolate.

"Doesn't he stink, though?" said Jess, more cheerfully after a couple of mouthfuls. "I can still smell it down here. What are my mates going to say? They won't want anything to do with me."

Mum suddenly got up from the table and crouched down on the floor. Jess was startled. This was no time for animal impersonations.

"Mum! What are you doing?" asked Jess. She felt her mum gingerly touch her left shoe. Mum reemerged, looking triumphant but disgusted.

"So much for Edouard smelling of dog poo," she said. "It's on your shoe, as a matter of fact."

Jess leapt to her feet in horror and examined her shoes. Mum was right! There was a horrid . . . well, never mind the details. This is what came of milling about in the dark, and not being able to see where you were going. Hastily Jess removed both shoes.

"Clean it off! Clean it off!" she begged.

"You're perfectly capable of cleaning it off yourself," said Mum. "But I've got a deal. I'll clean your shoes if you promise to be nice and friendly to Edouard for the next fortnight."

It hardly seemed fair. Being friendly to Edouard would be two weeks' backbreaking hard slog. Cleaning the shoes would probably only take five minutes. But faced with the horrible intensity of the pong, Jess agreed.

Later, just before she drifted off to sleep, Jess realized the ghastly fact that, just as she had assumed that Edouard smelt disgusting, Edouard's first impression of her would have been that *she* did. The only difference was that she really *had*. It was not the greatest start to their relationship.

10

"Go and wake him up, Jess." Mum was laying the table. She had bought some croissants specially for Edouard, but now she was worried that they might be a bit stale. She sniffed them suspiciously, then put them in the microwave.

"*Me* go and wake him up?" said Jess. "What, go in his bedroom and shake him or something?"

"Don't be silly," snapped Mum. "Just knock on the door and shout."

"Shout what?"

"Shout 'Edouard, wake up, it's seven o'clock.' Poor little chap," said Mum, sighing tragically. "He must be so tired."

"What about me? I'm *shattered!*" said Jess. She went upstairs. It seemed hard work. Each step was a mountain to climb. And this was going to go on for a whole two weeks. She paused outside Edouard's door. Her heart was thudding. She knocked. There was no reply.

"Edouard!" she called. "It's seven o'clock! Breakfast's ready!"

There was an answering squeak and a scuffle within. Jess bolted back downstairs.

"Is he awake?" asked Mum, taking the croissants out of the microwave and sniffing them again.

"Well, he's squeaking," said Jess. "I'm sure he'll be down in a minute. The smell of your magnificent croissants will lure him out of his den."

A few moments later they heard Edouard come out of his room and go into the bathroom.

"Thank God he's still alive," said Mum. "Wouldn't it be terrible if somebody's child died while they were staying with you?" Jess didn't answer. Yes, it would be awful—in theory. But she could think of some advantages. She hoped that if Edouard was thinking of dying, he'd get on with it right away and avoid days, even weeks, of needless torment.

"Can I have a croissant, Mum?" she asked. "They're getting cold again."

"*No!*—Oh, all right, then," said Mum, looking frazzled. Hospitality was not her strong point. "Do you think I should put them in a warm oven till he comes down? Yes, have one, and tell me how they taste."

Jess devoured a croissant in three enormous bites.

"Fine! Just relax, Mum. They're delicious," she said.

"There's ordinary bread as well, anyway. Everything's going to be just dandy." Jess didn't like to see her mum panicking. That was *her* job.

The bathroom was directly above the kitchen, and they could hear Edouard moving about. He tried to flush the loo. He tried again. Feebly. It didn't work. Again he tried. There was a pause. Again and again he cranked the handle, but he just couldn't get the thing to deliver.

Jess and her mum listened in frozen horror. Jess felt herself go cold all over. For a moment she imagined what it would be like to be in a strange house and not be able to flush the loo.

"Mum! You should have told him about the loo!" she hissed.

"Why do I have to do everything?" asked Mum, looking guilty. "I'll put a notice up."

"Too damn late," said Jess grimly. "Why do we have to have such a stupid loo anyway? Why can't we have a new one with an electronic flush you can set off with a mere flick of the finger? Why do we have to, like, hurl ourselves at the thing and throw all our weight on the handle? Our loo is retarded."

They heard Edouard give up on the loo and turn the washbasin taps on. Mum tried a feeble smile.

"Well, at least he's having a wash," she said.

"Terrific!" snarled Jess.

"You can show him how to flush the loo tonight," said Mum.

"I'm not showing him!" snapped Jess. "You're the parent, you do it! You're so irresponsible sometimes."

"I wouldn't talk to me in that tone of voice if I were you," said Mum, sounding dangerously brittle. "I could easily withdraw my goodwill and refuse to speak French to him. That would really drop you in it."

Eventually Edouard appeared, sat at the table, and ate two slices of bread with jam. He declined eggs, bacon, tea, orange juice, and worst of all, the croissants.

"Never mind," said Mum briskly. "More for us." She polished the last one off herself, but you could see she was hurt. "I must be careful not to descend into comfort eating," she added anxiously.

"Go for it, Mum," said Jess. "I'll join you. It might be the only way to get through this stinking fortnight." Then she turned to Edouard, gave him the sweetest of smiles, and offered him more milk. He was drinking milk, like a baby, though not from a bottle—not yet, anyway.

Mum drove them to school, talking to Edouard in French all the way. Jess sat in the backseat, happy to switch off. OK, her mum was a spineless nerd at times, but thank God for her gift with languages. At school, Edouard left Jess's side without a word and headed for the gang of French kids.

Flora came up with Marie-Louise by her side. They were both smiling. Jess felt a sharp pang of envy. Why, oh why, hadn't she asked for a girl? She'd hoped to land a handsome hunk—Edouard's photo had even made him look like one—but she'd ended up with a mere child. Now probably everyone at school was going to take the piss. Jokes about cradle snatching would be her sad destiny.

"Hi, Jess—this is Marie-Louise," said Flora. "Marie-Louise,

this is Jess." Marie-Louise beamed, seized Jess's hand, and kissed her quite bouncily on each cheek.

"I h'am very 'appy to meet you, Jess," she said. "I 'ave 'eard a lot about you!"

"You speak brilliant English!" said Jess. "Edouard hasn't said a word of English yet."

"Ah yes!" said Marie-Louise. "Edouard is your partner, isn't he? I must tell you a secret, Jess." She leant in close to Jess, her eyes dancing with fun. "Edouard 'as a very big crush on you! Yes! Since you sent him ze beautiful photo, he is looking at it all day. We 'ave been teazzing him!" She laughed.

A cold feeling of absolute horror spread through Jess's stomach. For a moment she thought she was going to be sick. It was bad enough that Edouard looked about ten years old. Worse, he apparently doted on her in an unattractive infantile way. She would never live this down.

"So you've pulled, babe!" said Flora, with a grin. "Well done! I always said you were irresistible!"

Jess panicked. She had to get out of this trap. A horrid nursery rhyme came into her head from nowhere: *Mary had a little lamb, Its fleece was white as snow, And everywhere that Mary went, That lamb was sure to go.*

She had a kind of wide-awake nightmare in which she was Mary and Edouard was the lamb, complete with wool and little black hooves. He trotted after her, bleating pathetically, a pink bow round his neck, his eyes shining in a grotesque lovesick manner behind his cute little glasses.

"What a shame!" Jess sort of exploded out of the hallucination and grasped wildly at something—anything—that would offer an escape. "Because I've already got a boyfriend." Flora looked amazed and puzzled, but luckily Marie-Louise didn't notice. "Fred and I are an item. We're practically engaged."

Flora, standing slightly behind Marie-Louise, looked over her shoulder at Jess and silently and hilariously mouthed *"Fred???!!"* Jess gave Flora a stern look, warning her not to rock the boat.

"I'm really sorry about Edouard," Jess went on. "I didn't encourage him or anything, I just sent him my photo." Well, that was almost true. The photo had been digitally enhanced to make her look irresistible, of course, but so what?

"Here comes Fred, now," said Flora, sniggering in an irritating way. "Jess's fiancé—well, nearly."

Fred was indeed gangling towards them, his hair sticking up foolishly, as if he hadn't combed it since he got up. Never mind. He might have been a ludicrous, panicky choice as honorary boyfriend, but at least he was tall.

Jess went over to him immediately, grabbed his tie, and looked up into his face.

"Try and look pleased to see me," she hissed. "From now we're officially going out together. Just for the next fortnight."

"What?" said Fred, going rather pale. "Nothing personal, but I'd rather eat a dead dog—without ketchup."

"Don't worry," said Jess. "You won't have to kiss me or anything gross. It's just that, to protect my honor, I have to have a pretend boyfriend while Edouard's here, and you were the first guy who came into my head."

"Fred tried to look flattered," said Fred. "But he was secretly making plans to flee to South America."

Jess looked across at the crowd of French students. Edouard had his back to her, but one or two of the others were looking across.

"Come on, Parsons!" she hissed. "Do this one little thing for me. Try to conquer your revulsion and be attentive. Win an Oscar."

Fred backed off, but Jess held on tight to his tie. Would Fred play ball, or would she have to strangle him first? He was so unpredictable. Maybe she should have said something else to put Edouard off. Maybe she should have said she was a lesbian. Oh well. If Fred messed up, Jess decided she might just have to become a gay icon overnight.

"Now listen, Fred!" said Jess. "We've got to walk past the French kids holding hands. Or at least ogling each other."

"Will the torment never cease?" said Fred. "I would rather eat a whole porcupine—raw." And he ran off.

Jess chased him, trying to laugh and make it all look terribly flirtatious. Their own mates looked amused. Most of them didn't know what was going on. But Jess Jordan and Fred Parsons had provided many a hilarious novelty over the years. Maybe this was their latest comedy stunt.

Whizzer, seeing Fred fleeing, deliberately stepped into his

path and grabbed him. Fred struggled, cursing. Whizzer held on tight with his large thuglike arms.

"Let him go, Whizzer," said Jess. "No need for mindless violence."

"Shall I nut 'im for you, darlin'?" asked the revolting Whizzer, leering at Jess.

"No, thank you," said Jess.

"Do you want to be her boyfriend for a fortnight?" said Fred, still trying to escape from Whizzer's meaty hands.

"What? Yeah! What's it, like a dare or somefing?" said Whizzer.

"Fred's just trying to escape from his responsibilities!" said Jess. "I'm expecting our first child!" Whizzer looked startled, let go of Fred, and backed off, shocked, amazed, and incredulous.

"What shall we call our first baby?" demanded Jess, loudly enough for the French to hear. Fred was retrieving his bag from the ground.

"Don't try and drag me into it," said Fred. "I can't even think of a name for my gerbil, and he's been dead for two years."

"Do you think the name Adolf will ever come back into fashion?" asked Jess. "Adolf Parsons . . . it has a certain ring."

"I'm not going to have children," said Fred. "I'm not even going to have another gerbil. The school fees were punishing."

They walked into school and waded into an immense sea of pupils milling around in the main lobby.

"Fred, you were hopeless," said Jess. "Is it too much to ask? That you just smile indulgently at me for once in your life?"

"I would rather walk barefoot through a trough of slugs," said Fred, "than go out with you for a split second. I have my reputation to think of."

"Your reputation could only be enhanced by a rumor that you were my beau," said Jess.

"Alas, no," said Fred. "My identity is based on solitude and eccentricity. I am what they call the 'ragged philosopher' type."

"What's the point of that?" asked Jess. "What ragged philosopher? He sounds like a loser."

"My mum took me to a homeopath once when I had a cough," said Fred. "And the homeopath said I was the 'ragged philosopher' type. I have my own homeopathic remedy. It's sulphur. I sprinkle it on my sandwiches."

Just then the French kids came past in a gang and were led away by a French teacher. Jess smiled as they passed, but Edouard didn't smile back. He only gave her a strange nod.

"He's such a little sweetie," said Fred. "I don't see what the problem is. Surely there are huge advantages in having a boyfriend who can fit in a matchbox. You could take him on holiday with you without your parents even knowing."

Jess just felt sick. Before Edouard had arrived, she'd been fantasizing about spending hours alone with him—even taking him off for a romantic weekend in St. Ives. Now even passing him in the school corridor seemed like an angsty ordeal.

The bell went, bringing an end to the horror and replacing it with geography. Normally Jess hated geography, with its dreary maps of coalfields and wretched climatic zones. But today it seemed almost like a holiday, compared with the awful drudgery of having a French exchange partner around. Jess drew a map of ocean currents without even feeling the faintest twinge of boredom. Perhaps she was going mad. Oh well. It would save time later.

Most of the time, the French students had separate lessons with their own teachers. In the French lesson, however, just before lunch, they had a big meeting. The French kids sat at one side of the room and the English kids at the other side.

Mrs. Bailey stood at one side of the teacher's desk and the French teacher, who was called Madame Lamentin, stood at the other.

"Mrs. Bailey's marginally better-looking," whispered Flora. "Lamentin's got warts."

Jess sneaked a peek at Edouard, but luckily he was not in the mood for eye contact. By now Marie-Louise must have told Edouard the news that Jess and Fred were an item. It must have been a crushing blow for the boy with the crush. Irritating though he was, Jess hoped that his little heart wasn't too broken at the discovery that she was nearly engaged.

"Right," said Mrs. Bailey, "may I welcome our French friends to Ashcroft School." She turned to them and gave a sickening smile. Mrs. Bailey's teeth were as crooked as a Neolithic stone circle. Maybe when she'd been young, orthodontic braces hadn't been invented.

"As you know, for this last week of term, most of the time the French students will be having their own lessons with Madame Lamentin. On Tuesday they will have an all-day trip to Stratford-on-Avon, and on Thursday they will have a day trip to London."

Thursday = bliss, Jess wrote on her notepad, adding a smiley face.

Gerard = Sex God? Flora scribbled. She was looking across at the French gang.

Jess followed her gaze. The French have a reputation for being good-looking, charismatic, and devilishly sexy. But, to be honest, Jess wouldn't have given most of them more than five out of ten. Not that the Brits were any better-looking—apart from Flora.

Gerard, Jodie's partner, was lounging rather attractively on his desk, and instead of looking politely at Mrs. Bailey, he appeared to be eyeing up the English girls on the opposite side of the room.

Up himself, wrote Jess, adding an obscene drawing of Gerard tied in a kind of knot, with his head buried in his backside. Flora got the giggles. Jodie, who was sitting in front of Jess and Flora, turned round and raised her eyebrows quizzically.

No love bites on Jodie, wrote Flora.

YET . . . wrote Jess. She drew a cartoon of Jodie covered with bruises, like a leopard.

Jess wondered whether anybody else in the English class would end up with French love bites. At least she'd be safe, as Fred's token girlfriend. Some boys (Whizzer for instance) would have made the most of the opportunity and been all over her.

But Fred was kind of weird. Jess had a feeling that Fred might reach the age of forty without sinking his teeth in anybody's neck. Except, possibly, in a vampire play. Fred was a complete mystery and could easily ruin the whole thing with some bizarre act of defiance. Jess would just have to keep her fingers crossed.

✳ 12 ✳

*A*t lunch the two groups began to mix. Jess was feeling a bit more relaxed, as apart from a few predictable jokes about Hobbits, nobody had given her a hard time about Edouard being a midget. You could see how, in his photo, Edouard had managed to look gorgeous. He did have good features, and one day might become something of a sex god, with one hell of a growth spurt and laser eye surgery.

In the absence of real teachers, Marie-Louise was like a kind of leader of the French gang. She sat down next to Flora and beckoned the other French kids to follow. Gerard swanned over wearing sunglasses. What a poser.

Jodie made sure he sat beside her, and fussed over him in a territorial way. The message was clear: *I'm having first crack at Gerard, so the rest of you keep your distance.*

"*Viens*, Edouard!" called Marie-Louise. Jess beckoned him over, too. She was sitting next to Fred, but they'd saved the seat for Edouard. He came over, carrying a plate of chips, and sat down opposite Jess without looking at her. Once he was settled, she said, "Edouard—this is my friend Flora, and my boyfriend Fred."

Edouard shook hands with them, said, "'Allo!" and gave a tight little smile. *Aaaah!* thought Jess. *Bless! He's being so brave!* She was starting to like him, as one might grow fond of a field mouse or pet canary. Jess hoped the discovery that Fred was her "boyfriend" would cure Edouard of his crush. Although maybe he had got over it the moment he saw the real Jess, in daylight.

"I hear you're going to be an engineer," said Fred in a strange voice. Jess realized he was impersonating one of the characters in the TV comedy series *Little Britain*—a posh, pervy old actor. Edouard frowned and clearly panicked. Conversation in English seemed beyond him. He turned to Marie-Louise and said something in French.

Marie-Louise translated for him, and he smiled back at Fred and unleashed a torrent of French.

"He says he is very interested in ze bridges," said Marie-Louise. "To build ze bridges and ze tunnels and so on."

"Well, if we ever need a bridge built, we'll come to you!" said Fred. He turned to Jess. "Do we need a bridge, wife? Possibly between the sofa and the fridge?" Everybody laughed. Marie-Louise translated for Edouard, who grinned, but in a slightly defensive way, as if he thought Fred was taking the piss.

"Right, then," said Fred. "I'm going to eat my own weight in baked beans, and then I'm going to enjoy a brief spell of wife-beating before maths."

"Don't bother to translate that," said Jess to Marie-Louise. "Fred's just being silly." She was beginning to feel safe now. Fred was, in his own ludicrous way, pretending to be her boyfriend. She could relax. It was working—sort of.

"So," said Marie-Louise, "how long 'ave you two been going out togezzer?"

"Oh, for years," said Jess.

"Oh, since last Sunday," said Fred—the idiot. Jess blushed. It seemed a bit early to relax after all.

"Never believe a word Fred says about anything," she said. "He's just trying to make me look a fool."

"You can do that yourself, sweetie," said Fred, "without any help from me."

"So," said Marie-Louise, "tell me all about it. 'Ow you met, 'ow you got togezzer . . . ?"

Jess took a huge breath. She was going to have to dig deep. She kicked Fred under the table, as a sign he should shut up. But would he?

"We met at playgroup," she said. "We were about three years old or something. We had a fight over an inflatable bus."

"So . . . ," Marie-Louise said, "you 'ave been togezzer for twelve years?"

"Yes," said Jess, surprised to discover just how long she

had known Fred. The bit about the playgroup was all true. "But Fred's still three years old in some ways."

"I still hurl sand about and dribble gravy down my shirt," admitted Fred.

"And do your parents get on wiz each other?" asked Marie-Louise. She was beginning to be a bit tedious. What was she, a premarriage guidance counselor?

"Oh, my mum hates Fred," said Jess. "She can't stand the way he spits when he talks. And she would have preferred me to have a sporty boyfriend. Joe Collins, the rugby captain, or something."

"Ah!" said Marie-Louise, clapping her hands. "I adore ze rugby!"

"Oh yes!" said Flora. "The French rugby team is brilliant. I know cos my dad watches it on TV all the time. Maybe we could all go to a match together this weekend?"

"Great idea!" said Jodie, barging in rugby-style. "Do you like rugby, Gerard?"

"Bof!" said Gerard, and shrugged.

"We'll take that as a *no*, then," said Fred. "Anyway, there aren't any rugby matches this weekend. It's almost the end of the season."

"It would be nice, though, to go somewhere, all of us together," said Flora thoughtfully.

Too right, thought Jess. Apparently there wasn't anything special laid on for the French kids this weekend. They were supposed to enjoy "quality time with their host families," according to Mrs. Bailey's schedule. Jess couldn't imagine getting through a weekend at home, just her, Mum, and

Edouard, without them all going stark raving mad in separate rooms, hiding under their duvets and silently eating their pillows. Some kind of communal event would certainly help pass the time. It was a lot easier getting along with Edouard when there were plenty of other people around.

"I know!" said Flora. "We could go camping!"

"Excuse me!?" said Jess. "Did you say *camping*? You've never been camping in your life."

"I know, but I've always wanted to!" said Flora. "My mum always insists on staying in hotels, but I'd absolutely *adore* to go camping."

"Camping!" cried Marie-Louise. "It's really a marvelous idea!"

"But it'll be freezing!" said Jess, who *had* been camping once, in Wales, in the rain, with a mum who was having a migraine.

"We can have a campfire!" said Flora. That did sound rather attractive. "And besides," Flora went on, "my dad was talking about the weather yesterday, and apparently there's going to be a mini–heat wave at the weekend. Perfect for camping."

"Where would we go, though?" said Jess.

"My auntie Rose lives on a farm," said Jodie. "She's got loads of fields."

"It would have to have a shower block, and toilets," said Fred. "I'm not urinating behind any hedges."

"Don't say urinating," hissed Jess. "It sounds mank."

"If we went to my auntie's," said Jodie, "we could use her downstairs bathroom. And they've got an outside loo."

"It would be bliss to get away from my dad for a few hours," sighed Flora. "He's always showing off, speaking French and waving his arms about."

Jess privately agreed. OK, camping might be a bit cold and weird, but it would be great to get away from fussing old parents for a while. This camping idea was growing on her.

Edouard, who had been trying to follow the conversation while eating his chips, asked Marie-Louise something in French. She explained, and Edouard looked surprised, then pleased, then suddenly worried. It was strange, how many facial expressions he had when talking French. At home, his face was a numb mask of torment.

"What's the problem?" asked Jess.

"Edouard is worrying about his hay fever," said Marie-Louise. "But I told him it is too early in ze year. Zere will be no—how you say?"

"Pollen," said Fred. "A lovely name for a gerbil, now I come to think of it."

Marie-Louise seemed deep in thought for a minute. She looked at Fred, and then at Jess, and then she turned and whispered something to Flora. It was so obviously something about Fred and Jess. Flora whispered back, but she looked amused, and afterwards she gave Jess a secret little look which meant that she would tell her later, and they would crack up.

Later had to be in the loos, because whenever they had any free time, Edouard and Marie-Louise were always tagging along.

"We've lost our privacy," Jess hissed, as they washed their

hands at adjacent basins. "The goddamn frogs are always around. What was M-L saying about me?"

"She said she'd heard a rumor you were preggers!" Flora replied, giggling. "I soon put her straight about that."

"Right!" said Jess. "I hope you told her I was the Virgin Queen of Ashcroft School, and planning to stay that way."

"M-L is like a parent," said Flora thoughtfully. "She's kind of middle-aged. But really nice."

"The camping idea is brilliant!" said Jess. "Only problem is, we haven't got a tent, let alone two."

"Why two?" asked Flora.

"One for me and one for Edouard. I'm not sharing with him! He gives me the creeps."

"I think he's rather sweet," said Flora. "I like short guys anyway. They're less threatening."

They were now slightly late for English, and had to run. At the corner by the gym, they bumped into the history teacher, Miss Dingle (known as Dingbat, obviously).

"Jess Jordan!" she cried, and Jess skidded to a halt. "Where's that essay you owe me about Charles the First?"

Jess wondered, fleetingly, why she was always the one to get into trouble. It was going to be one of those days.

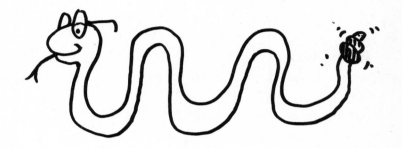

*J*ess ended up with some extra history homework as well as the Charles I essay, thanks to Miss Dingle's PMS.

"Although," said Jess as they packed up their bags at the end of the day, "I'd almost rather do extra homework than have to spend time with my little friend from across the sea."

"I'm really lucky," admitted Flora. "Marie-Louise speaks better English than I do. If I was alone with somebody shy and speechless like Edouard I'd totally freak out."

At this point the French gang arrived. Gerard, Jodie's

partner, was wearing shades, and he strolled up to Jess and Flora.

"'Ave you seen Jodie?" he asked.

"She'll be here in a minute," said Flora. "Have you had a good day?"

Gerard shrugged and sort of pouted as if to suggest that his first day in England had been not particularly wonderful. Tolerable, maybe.

"Bof!" he said. Or something similar.

"Couldn't agree more," said Jess. "My day was totally bof as well."

Gerard took off his shades, looked at Jess for a moment, and grinned slowly.

"You are fanny," he said in a drawly sort of voice. His green eyes sort of smoldered.

"No, fortunately, I'm Jess," said Jess. "Here's Jodie now." She didn't want to get on the wrong side of Jodie by flirting with Gerard. Jodie had once thrown a whole set of PE kit at Amber Forsyth's head, just because Amber had said something that upset Jodie slightly.

Jodie rushed in looking panicky that her precious Gerard was daring to talk to other girls. He gave Jodie a very seductive welcoming smile. She blushed so hard that, for a moment, all her spots disappeared.

"Come on, Gerard!" she said. "My mum will be waiting— oh, by the way," she added, in a kind of public announcement sort of voice, "I'll sort out the camping trip with my auntie Rose, no problem." There was a cheer.

Jodie's certainly Queen Bee at the moment, thought Jess.

Marie-Louise bustled up to Flora. "Oh, I 'ave 'ad such a simply wonderful day!" she said. "Madame Lamentin show us a video about British 'istory avec Simon Schama. Ze Middle Ages. I love zis! Tomorrow we are going to Oxford. I am so excited!"

Bless her, thought Jess. *Fancy getting off on the Middle Ages. Maybe it's because she's so middle-aged.*

Flora and Marie-Louise went off home, and moments later Jess was wishing that she could have had a partner like that. Edouard crept towards her, staring sadly at the floor as if he was too embarrassed to look her in the eye. His crush— if he'd ever had one—was certainly crushed.

"We're going to walk home," she said. "It's not far."

Edouard nodded seriously. Jess's heart sank. Then, suddenly, Fred appeared, grinning.

"Hi, Ed!" he said, slapping Edouard affectionately on the back. Edouard produced a shy smile. "How's it going?" said Fred. "Do you fancy being engaged to Jess for a bit? I'm bored with it already."

"He can't understand that much English," said Jess, laughing. Edouard laughed, too, and shrugged.

"Jess—dog!" said Fred, making a barking sound. Edouard laughed.

"Fred—pig!" said Jess, snorting piggishly. Edouard laughed again.

"What Edouard?" asked Fred. Edouard paused for thought.

"Edouard—snake!" said Edouard eventually, and gave a brief and rather surprising hiss.

"Laugh? We nearly did!" said Fred. "I'll walk you both home, as long as I don't have to hold hands with you. I'd rather hold hands with your friend."

"God, you're all over me all the time," said Jess. "Keep your distance, can't you, Parsons? And by the way, Mum and I usually refer to you-know-who as the Queen."

They set off, and immediately it became awkward. There was only room for two people to walk side by side on the pavement. Edouard immediately dropped back behind Jess and Fred.

"This is awful," said Jess. "The Queen seems kind of sad and neglected." She stopped and turned. Edouard, who had been looking at the ground, bumped into her, and his glasses went crooked.

"Sorry," said Jess.

"Sorry," said Edouard, blushing.

"Fred wants to talk to you about something," said Jess, indicating that Edouard ought to walk in front in a boys-bonding kind of way.

"Er—what was it I wanted to talk to him about, again?" said Fred.

"Oh God, anything," said Jess.

"What sort of music do you like, Ed?" asked Fred. Edouard looked panicky—even from behind.

"La musique," said Fred. "Coldplay? Madonna? Nirvana? Beethoven?"

Eventually Edouard realized what Fred was talking about, and joined in. At one point Fred looked over his shoulder and said, "Ed and I share a passion for Fat Chance."

"Excellent!" said Jess. "Keep up the good work!"

It was so much easier getting through half an hour with Edouard if somebody else was there. She prayed that her mum would be home already when they got back.

But Mum's car wasn't parked outside as usual. Maybe there had been some kind of holdup at the library. "For God's sake, don't leave me alone with the Queen," she begged, as she unlocked the front door. Fred was loitering by the gate. He began to put on his I'm-off-now face. "He'll try it on with me the moment your back's turned," said Jess, at speed. "As my fiancé, you should be a tad more possessive."

Fred gave a charming, treacherous smile, shrugged his shoulders, and backed away.

"So much homework," he said. "So little time . . ." Then, abruptly, he blew her a sarcastic kiss and ran off.

Jess heaved a deep sigh and turned to face Edouard. This time there was no escape.

There was a note on the hall table. Edouard hesitated for a moment, then ran upstairs. Jess heard his bedroom door close as she read the message from Mum.

Jess, I'm sorry, but I won't be home till very late today—probably about midnight. I've had to go off to Granny's. Nothing to worry about. I've just got to go and check on something. There's a pizza in the freezer and some ice cream. Sorry to leave you in the lurch on Edouard's first evening, but I'm sure you'll cope.

Jess slammed the note down in total disgust. What on earth was this Granny crisis? If it wasn't serious or anything to worry about, why had Mum dashed off on a long journey just like that? It took nearly two hours to get to Granny's. Jess's stomach seemed to writhe inside her like a living snake.

She went to the fridge and got herself a glass of juice. Maybe she should get Edouard one, too. Suddenly she heard him come out of his room, and she braced herself. Oh God! What if he said something? In French? If only she had paid attention in French lessons instead of making secret drawings of the Perfect Boy (hair of Eminem, smile of David Beckham, eyes of Joaquin Phoenix, etc.).

But thanks be to God! Edouard went into the bathroom and locked the door. But wait! What if he was ill or something? What could be worse than having to be sick in a foreign language? Or having diarrhea and knowing the host family could hear your groans? Jess flew to the TV and turned it on very loud. She found *The Simpsons*. It blotted out all other sounds. Jess tried to sit and watch it for a while, but she couldn't concentrate. Even the cleverest and funniest TV program in the world couldn't distract her from her massive ordeal. A French boy upstairs.

After a while, she heard Edouard trying to flush the loo again. Oh no! They hadn't had time to show him how to do it, yet. There hadn't been a spare moment to fix up a tactful little sign: PLEASE TAKE A RUNNING JUMP AND HURL YOUR-SELF BODILY ONTO THE LOO HANDLE. *Please take a running jump anyway,* thought Jess.

Edouard went on cranking away for ages like some kind of demented piece of farm machinery. Jess turned the TV sound up even more and stuffed her fingers in her ears. Eventually, she sensed movement above and heard Edouard go back into his room and shut the door.

Part of her wanted him to stay there for the rest of eternity. But part of her wanted him to come bounding cheerfully downstairs and say, "Right, babe, what's for supper? Get that grub on the table, gal!" (In a French accent, of course.) However, right now it seemed that the former of these two possibilities was more likely than the latter. Would Edouard and Jess ever commit communication? She doubted it.

Jess stared blankly at *The Simpsons* for a while, her mind racing. Then she began to tune into it and enjoy it. Time passed. After a short eternity of entertainment, she became uneasily aware that Edouard had still not come downstairs yet. She wondered if he ever would. Much as she dreaded his coming downstairs, if he didn't she would be in big trouble. He had to eat. What if he died of starvation? It would be in the papers and everything. Her mum might even go to prison.

She turned the TV sound down and walked to the bottom of the stairs. She would call him and ask him if he liked pizza. That couldn't be too difficult. She opened her mouth. No sound came out. She shuddered and felt sick. She opened her mouth again. A tiny squeak came out.

Jess went back into the sitting room and sat down. Her heart was thumping. This was ridiculous! How could it be so hard just to give a boy a pizza? She went into the kitchen, picked up the phone, and dialed Flora's number. Her dad picked up.

"Barclay!" he barked. Jess cringed. Flora's dad was so frightening.

"Hi, is Flora there?" she asked, in a small, inoffensive, insectlike voice.

"Who is that?" demanded Mr. Barclay.

"It's—er, Jess," said Jess, for a moment forgetting her own name, so great was her terror of this international business-man. Mr. Barclay imported bathrooms and was always nip-ping off to Milan to inspect bidets.

"Look, Jess. Just identify yourself when you ring peo-ple up, OK? It saves time. Flora can't come to the phone right now. We're in the middle of supper. She'll call you back later."

"Sorry, sorry!" said Jess. She was deeply regretting phon-ing Flora. Thank God her own dad was feeble and lived hundreds of miles away. She couldn't cope with all this sergeant-major stuff.

"I just wanted to ask what the French was for 'Do you like pizza?'" said Jess.

"*How* many years have you been doing French?" de-manded Mr. Barclay. He sighed in a self-important, sarcastic way. "Oh well, never mind. It's *Aimez-vous pizza?* Or, if you want it in Italian, *Lei vuole pizza?*"

"Thank you," said Jess. "Didn't mean to disturb you. Sorry. Thanks you very much."

She rang off in confusion. She had said, "Thanks you very much"! Oh God! He would think she was a retard! She had been going to say "Thanks," but then it had started to sound too casual, and she'd decided, at the last minute, to change it to "Thank you very much," but she hadn't quite managed it.

Still, at least she now knew the French for "Do you like pizza?" What was it again? Jess's brain whirled. She felt as if she might faint. The horror of her phone call to Mr. Barclay had blotted out the actual French words he'd told her. All she could remember was the vague sound of the Italian version, which he'd insisted on telling her as well—the big-head! Something sounding like "vole."

Vole pizza. What a ghastly image it conjured up. Limp with effort, Jess dragged herself across the kitchen and opened the door of the freezer. There was indeed a pizza in there. She got it out. It stuck to her fingers, burning with cold. Even inanimate objects seemed hostile and threatening tonight. She brushed the pizza off her fingers. It clattered down onto the table. She peered at it through its coat of frost. The freezer needed defrosting, as ever—it was like Antarctica in there. However, there didn't appear to be any dead voles on the pizza. One small triumph in the nightmare of this endless evening.

She walked to the bottom of the stairs and listened. No sound. Was he dead? She almost hoped so. She just had to call him. She opened her mouth, filled her lungs, and plucked up her courage.

"Edouard!" she called. Her voice sounded thin and weedy, but it was definitely loud enough to be heard. There was no reply. Jess was astonished. She had expected him to come straight to the door. A spear of fear went straight through her tummy. "Edouard!" she called again, louder. Still no reply. Still absolutely no sound or movement upstairs.

Jess began to feel annoyed. Why the hell couldn't he just answer to his name? Even very stupid dogs could do that. She felt a fool, standing there and yelling. She decided she wouldn't call him anymore. She would pretend she had been singing. Edouard, the way they pronounced it in French—*Ed waaaagh*—sounded just a tiny bit like "It was." Jess remembered a song her father always sang. "*It was just one of those things, just one of those crazy flings . . .*"

She walked away from the stairs singing "*Edouard just one of those things . . .*" She arrived in the kitchen, singing with deranged fury, and decided she was hungry. She'd just cook the damn pizza, and if Edouard didn't appear she'd eat it all herself. She switched the oven on with furious panache, and hurt herself quite badly on the switch.

The oven leapt into life. Its reassuring hum was like the voice of a long-lost friend. Jess ripped the wrapper off the pizza. Soon the most delicious smell was wafting through the house. And suddenly, there was a sound from upstairs. Lured by the whiff of cheese and tomato, Edouard was leaving his room! Jess's heart started to beat fast. Any minute now she would be required to speak French.

She heard Edouard start coming downstairs. But there was an awful sickening stumble, a strange squeaking French kind of gasp, a thump, more thumps and thuds, and the unmistakable sound of a small French boy actually falling downstairs! Oh my God! Maybe this time he really had died.

* 15 *

*J*ess was tempted for a moment to turn tail and run out into the garden. She could hide behind some bushes down at the bottom, by the picnic table, until Edouard had gone away. Or been taken away by ambulance. Or possibly the funeral director.

She hovered, desperate, by the kitchen door. What should she do? On the one hand, she ought to run and see if he was all right. On the other hand, if she'd fallen downstairs in his house, she would have preferred it if nobody saw.

There was a rustling sound out in the hall. He wasn't dead or unconscious, then. Jess crept hesitantly out of the kitchen. Edouard was scrambling to his feet. His back was to her, and, oh Lordy! His trousers were split right up the back! And for a fleeting second, she got a flash of his underpants, which were adorned with small red teddy bears.

Edouard turned towards her. It was almost like a moment from a film, in slow motion. He placed his hands behind him. Jess knew he was holding his trousers shut. Their eyes met. There was no possibility of a smile. Smiles were hundreds of miles away.

Jess just raised her eyebrows in what she hoped was a caring way—raised them so far that her scalp actually hurt.

"Pizza?" she said in a strange, demented croak. Edouard shrugged, while still holding on to the back of his trousers. Jess knew it would be polite to stand back and usher him into the kitchen first, but then she would have to see the back of his trousers. So instead she led the way in. She had laid two places at the kitchen table, and she got the pizza out of the oven.

Edouard sat down, with a faint ripping sound. The damage had evidently gone further. He was pale, and looked like a soul in deep torment. Jess wondered for an instant how you could say, in French, "I do hope you haven't hurt yourself while falling downstairs, and let me assure you that I didn't see your underpants, and sewing is my favorite hobby—just leave those trousers outside your bedroom door."

Actually she didn't think she'd ever manage to say anything like that even in English. She cut the pizza carefully in half, picked up Edouard's bit on a spatula, and headed for his plate. But what was this? Edouard was shaking his head and waving it away. What? He didn't want pizza?

"No pizza?" asked Jess incredulously.

"No pizza," confirmed Edouard, blushing and shaking his head. "Sank you."

Well, sank you, too, buddy, thought Jess. She placed the slice of pizza on her plate. Edouard just sat there, miserably looking at the salt and pepper mills. His plate was empty. Jess had to offer him something. She opened the fridge and got out some cheese, salami, ham, olives, the butter, the margarine, some French-type soft cream cheese with garlic, and a carton of orange juice.

She placed them all on the table in front of Edouard, who looked at them miserably and with revulsion, as if Jess had placed a decomposing dog in front of him. Jess was tempted, for a moment, to grab the rolling pin and—but no! He was a stranger in a foreign land! And he had teddy bears on his underpants. Remembering this detail, Jess felt a brief shiver of something like tenderness.

She got out the bread. Luckily it was already sliced. She found some crackers, some Ryvita, some hummus, some guacamole. She even put a pack of corn chips on the table, and opened a jar of salsa dip. Still Edouard gazed at the feast with what looked like dismay.

Jess foraged in the most remote and secret cupboards and found a packet of chocolate biscuits. She placed it before him. Edouard's expression modulated just a touch. His face made a faint transition from torment to mere anguish. He reached for a chocolate biscuit. Phew! Nourishment was being attempted.

Jess poured him a glass of juice, sat down, and started to eat her pizza. The silence was deafening. She began to notice the awful chewing noises she was making, and when she sipped her juice, it went *slurp—glug glug glug* in a most unattractive way. Mind you, Edouard wasn't any better. He was eating with his mouth open. It was like watching a cement mixer preparing to build a chocolate house.

Once she'd eaten half of the pizza, Jess wondered if she ought to eat the other half. If she didn't, it would just be lying there and Edouard might feel guilty that he'd rejected it. She damn well hoped he'd feel guilty, anyway. No! Think of the teddy bears frolicking on his bottom. He was a stranger in a foreign land.

After four chocolate biscuits and a sip of juice, Edouard cleared his throat. Jess plowed on with the second half of her pizza. It was hard work. She'd burnt it a bit, to be honest.

"Hmmm!" said Edouard, and wiped his mouth on the back of his hand. Oh no! He was going to speak.

"Wheretamare?" he said. It was so obviously a question. But what on earth did it mean?

"Sorry?" said Jess politely, raising her eyebrows and trying to look as if she just hadn't quite heard, rather than failing to understand.

"Wheretamare?" said Edouard again, the fool. It was so unfair of him to speak in French. He was supposed to be here to learn English.

"To be honest," said Jess, smiling pleasantly, "I haven't the faintest idea what you're rabbiting on about, but never mind." If only Flora and Fred were here to enjoy this kind of sarcastic game. Or even Mum.

However, Jess did remember vaguely that the French for "where" did sound quite like "where," though it was spelt . . . uhhh . . . *où est.* Bingo! Bravo! Perhaps even Bongo! So he was asking *where* something was.

But what? The mare? The female horse? Hmmm, unlikely. But wait . . . *mer*! Jess remembered now! *La mer* was "the sea." They'd done a bit of French geography recently, and Mrs. Bailey had pointed out that France was surrounded by three seas: the English Channel to the north, the Atlantic to the west, and the Med down south. But good old Britain still beat them hands down, with sea all round.

So . . . Edouard had apparently asked where the sea was. Was this a sign of suicidal thoughts? Had he plans to run to the shore and hurl himself in? And where the hell *was* the nearest sea? To Jess's intense disappointment, trips to the beach did not loom very large in her day-to-day life.

Her dad did live in St. Ives, which was by the sea, but that was hundreds of miles away and she hadn't actually been down there yet. She had a feeling that even the nearest sea to home was miles and miles away, or, as Edouard would probably prefer to think of it, kilometers. She smiled, nodded, and raised her finger as if to indicate he should speak no more. (And *how*.)

"*Où est la mer?*" she said, with a triumphant smile. Edouard nodded and almost smiled, too. Communication had been achieved!

"Hang on a tick," said Jess. "I'll just go and find an atlas!" She leapt to her feet. Edouard watched her, looking puzzled. She went off into the sitting room. It seemed unbearably delightful in there, empty and welcoming, with no

French exchange person waiting to be fed and talked to. Jess ransacked the bookshelves.

As her mum was a librarian, all the books were in perfect order. There was a whole section of atlases. Jess found them right away, but she pretended to have to look for a bit longer, so she could have a few more precious minutes on her own. Then she carried one back to the kitchen.

"The atlas!" she cried, as if atlases were the most fab fashion accessory. She plonked it down on the table. Edouard looked mystified. Jess flipped through the pages until she came to a map of their region. In the bottom right-hand corner was a bit of sea.

"There!" she said, grinning in triumph. Edouard stared at her as if she had gone insane. What the hell was wrong with the guy? He was the one who'd raised the subject of geography in the first place. Jess measured the distance from their home to the sea, using a convenient knife.

"What's the scale of this map?" she said, in a thoughtful kind of way, talking to herself. It was the only sensible thing, really. She was the only person in the room who could understand. Using the scale, she worked out that they lived about seventy-two miles from the sea.

"Seventy-two miles!" she announced. Edouard looked blank, even panicky. Jess knew it was the miles that were the problem.

"Come!" she said, and ran upstairs. Edouard followed slowly, holding his trousers shut at the back. Jess raced into her mum's study and went online. She dragged an extra chair alongside her for Edouard. He sat down with a faint ripping sound.

Jess tapped *miles-kilometers* into Google. She went to a site called EscapeArtist.com. Jess smiled at the irony of it. If only she could escape, right now! There was a conversion chart.

"There!" said Jess. "The sea is 115 kilometers away!" She expected Edouard to look pleased, but instead he looked lost and slightly tearful. Then Jess had her first good idea of the evening. She leapt up and offered Edouard the seat at the computer. He accepted it instantly, and jumped eagerly into the chair. His little fingers flew across the keyboard and Jess was amazed to see whole Web pages in French appearing. How amazing!

There seemed to be a lot of people being fabulous in French: kissing each other on both cheeks, watering chic pot plants in French, skiing, windsurfing, the lot. At the sight of his countrymen frolicking about Frenchly, Edouard started to look a bit happier. So Jess said, "Just going down to do the washing-up!" and escaped downstairs.

It was annoying having to do the washing-up, especially as she'd made the supper, but wasn't that just like a boy? After she'd cleared the table and burped several times (there had been too much pizza and she had violent indigestion), Jess decided to phone Flora again.

"Please God," she whispered as she dialed, "make it Flora who answers, not her dad." Although to be honest, sometimes Jess thought that perhaps Flora's dad *was* God. His voice was certainly loud enough.

✳ 16 ✳

La mère? La MER? Oh merde!

"ello?" Bliss! It was Flora's mum. She was a wonderful, cuddly, glamorous, lazy person who spent most of her time on the sofa. She always treated Jess like a long-lost extra daughter, whereas her husband always treated Jess like a broken bidet, fit only to be kicked.

Eventually, after sharing with Mrs. Barclay the trials and tribulations of being home alone with her French boy, Jess was reunited with Flora.

"How's it going, babe?" asked Flora. "We're having a great time. I'm redesigning Marie-Louise's eyebrows."

Suppressing a wave of jealousy (it should be Jess who was

receiving this kind of cosmetic attention), she cut straight to the crisis.

"It's a nightmare!" she said. "My mum's gone off to Granny's! He wouldn't eat the pizza! He's only had five chocolate biscuits! He fell downstairs and split his trousers and I saw his underpants! And he can't flush our loo and I'm too embarrassed to mention it—and even if I did, he wouldn't understand a word."

"Put a video on," advised Flora.

"It's all right—he's on the Internet at the moment," said Jess. "Did you know they have an Internet, too, all in French? It's weird."

"Well, let him surf away all night, then," said Flora. "At least it gets him out of your hair."

"What's the time?" asked Jess.

"Er—ten past seven."

"Only ten past seven?" screamed Jess in anguish. "How am I ever going to get through this evening?"

"Homework?" suggested Flora, who always did hers the moment she got home. (If she didn't, there was no supper, by order of God.)

"Homework!" said Jess. "Brilliant! Brilliant! I'll do my homework! And when I've done it all, I'll invent some more!"

"Edouard will have homework, too, don't forget," said Flora.

"Yeah! Of course! Brilliant! I always wondered what was the point of homework, but now it seems quite a wonderful invention," said Jess. "Oh, by the way, he asked me this really weird question—where's the sea?"

"The sea?" said Flora, puzzled.

"Yeah, like: *Où est la mer?* I looked it all up and everything. I even translated it into kilometers, but he just looked puzzled. God! He's so ungrateful. As well as being anorexic."

"It might not have been 'Where is the sea?'" said Flora, rather irritatingly. "It might have been 'Where is your mother?' You know: *Où est ta mère?*"

"But it sounds so similar," complained Jess, though light was beginning to dawn.

"One's got an extra 'e,'" said Flora. Jess, despite being grateful for the explanation, still wanted to hit Flora, slightly. "That would make sense, wouldn't it, as your mum's out?"

"That's it! That is so obviously it," said Jess. "Thanks. All I have to do now is translate into French: Mum's gone to see Granny for some unknown reason and she'll be back at midnight and sends her apologies. It'll only take seven weeks for me to do that, but hey! The evening's going to be that long anyway."

"Wait a min," said Flora. "I'll just ask Marie-Louise what it is."

Eventually Flora and Marie-Louise translated the message into French and dictated it to Jess, who wrote it down. She replaced the phone and heaved a massive sigh. Never mind homework. Her brain was totally exhausted already.

She went upstairs. Edouard was still checking his e-mails. Jess placed the slip of paper in front of him. Edouard read it, then turned towards her with something that was almost a smile, and nodded. Jess felt a tidal wave of relief wash over her. She went downstairs and got out her homework.

Never had homework seemed less boring. Even though she was already tired out, the prospect of having to make small talk with Edouard was even worse than having to write an essay about the Roundheads and the Cavaliers. Jess was herself a Cavalier, obviously, because she loved all the velvet and lace and curls and stuff. She also loved drama, and had hated the Roundheads ever since she discovered they'd closed all the theaters. She threw herself into the essay with panache.

Sometime during the trial of King Charles I, Edouard could be heard leaving the computer and going into the bathroom. There was a long silence, and then he started the loo-flushing routine. However, this time, after about seventeen attempts, when Jess was on the point of covering her ears and screaming aloud, he actually somehow made a huge effort and managed it.

It was music to Jess's ears. She sighed again, with relief this time. Then she heard Edouard coming out of the bathroom. She cringed in anticipation of him coming, or possibly falling, downstairs, but instead he did the decent thing: he went into his bedroom and closed the door.

Thanks be to God! Jess returned to her essay. It was so odd to be sitting at home willingly doing an essay without Mum standing behind her with her arms folded and wearing a ferocious scowl. Having a visitor changed everything.

Eventually she finished the essay (a Grade A, surely, this time—it was three and a half pages instead of her usual one and a half). Then Jess placed some corn chips, a tiny pot of dip, a banana, an apple, a piece of cheese, and three more chocolate biscuits on a plate and left them outside Edouard's door with a can of Coke. She knocked, and ran away downstairs. It was a bit like looking after a pet hedgehog.

After this act of charity she switched on the TV. She sprawled out full-length on the sofa, and the next thing she knew, Mum and Granny were staring down at her and something random to do with deep-sea fishing was on the telly. Jess realized she must have been asleep for hours. She hoped Edouard hadn't come downstairs and seen her. She sat up, yawned, and stretched.

"It's midnight," said Mum. "Come on, Jess. You can share my bed tonight. Granny's staying with us, just for a day or two. She can sleep in your room."

"Are you OK, Granny?" asked Jess, leaping up and giving her adored grandparent a hug.

"I'm fine, thank you, dear," said Granny. "But I've apparently got to be punished for my recent bad behavior."

"Don't be silly, Granny," said Jess's mum.

"What bad behavior?" asked Jess. Granny shrugged.

"Just talking to somebody," she said in a sarcastic tone of voice. "I won't intrude by taking your bed, dear," she said. "I'll just sleep right here on the sofa."

"No!" said Mum. "You'll sleep in Jess's bed! Please! You know it's for the best. I'll just go and get you a cup of cocoa."

Mum went off to the kitchen, and Granny sat down on the sofa, looking massively pissed off. Jess was amazed at this evidence of a row between the adults, but wondered if the best thing would be to distract her granny with small talk.

"So, Granny!" she said, grasping the old dear's hand. "Heard about any good murders recently?" Granny was an enthusiastic devotee of TV and newspaper homicide. Granny gave her an exasperated look, glinting with malice.

"I haven't heard of any, dear," she remarked. "But if things don't get any better I shall be committing one fairly soon."

My God! Her granny thinking about murdering her mum! What on earth was going on?

"So what on earth's going on with Granny?" asked Jess, once she was installed in Mum's double bed. Mum switched the light off.

"Nothing," she said. "It's not important."

"It seems pretty important," said Jess. "After all, you've dragged her all the way here and she seems totally gutted. What's happened? Has she been dating someone unsuitable?" Grandpa had been dead awhile now, and Jess had wondered if people as old as Granny ever fell in love a second time around.

"Don't be silly," said Mum. "Be quiet, now, Jess, please! I want to go to sleep. I'm shattered."

"I won't shut up until you tell me what it's all about," said Jess.

Mum sighed.

"Well, Granny's being exploited," said Mum.

"Exploited? How?"

"She's got a new friend—a woman called Gina."

"What's wrong with this Gina?" asked Jess. "Isn't Granny allowed to choose her own friends or something? That's a bit harsh. She's not a baby."

There was a long pause while Mum sat up and took two headache pills. She didn't have to switch the light on, because the bottle of water and the pills were always right there on her bedside table. Then she lay down again and pulled the covers up round her ears. Jess waited. Her mum said nothing.

"I said, what's wrong with this Gina?" demanded Jess.

"What's wrong with her is that Granny has to pay her twenty quid every time they have a talk!" snapped Mum.

"What?" Jess couldn't believe it. "You mean she charges Granny to have a conversation with her?"

"Yes," said Mum. "That's about the size of it. And they've been having three or four little conversations a week recently. It's just not on. I won't have my mum exploited. I'm going to sleep now, Jess. It's nearly half past twelve, for God's sake! We've got to be up at the crack of dawn to get Edouard off for his Oxford trip."

"Oh, by the way," said Jess, "he split his trousers this evening by falling downstairs."

"What?" Mum whirled round in bed so fast, she made

herself giddy. "Oh, my head! Horrid . . . It'll stop in a minute. . . . Did you say *fell downstairs*?"

"Yes," said Jess. "And it wasn't my fault. He did it all by himself."

"Was he hurt?" asked Mum.

"Well, he pretended it hadn't happened, so he can't have been hurt all that much."

"Oh God!" Mum shuddered. "What if he'd died?"

"Mum, he patently didn't die. He sat down in the kitchen and ate some supper, and then he checked his e-mails. Why don't you worry about the real crisis here: that his trousers are split right down the back? I actually saw a glimpse of his underpants. They had teddy bears on."

"How sweet!" said Mum thoughtfully. "Don't worry about the trousers. He's bound to have brought a couple of pairs at least. Granny can fetch them down and mend them tomorrow, while he's away."

"When's she going home?" asked Jess.

"When she sees sense," said Mum grimly. "Please stop talking now, Jess. I've got to get to sleep and so have you."

Jess, who had been asleep on the sofa already this evening, found it harder to nod off, but eventually she managed it.

In no time at all she was back at school. Oh God! She was late for registration. And a sudden horrible fear ran through her. Had she done her homework? Had she? Had she? She searched her bag. No homework! A bell rang. Oh no! She'd missed registration!

Gerard loomed up. They were surrounded by crowds of

people, but he gazed into her eyes, grabbed her, and crushed her to his manly chest.

"I love you, Jess," he said. Everybody standing around started applauding. It was embarrassing, but quite wonderful, too. Jess's heart soared with happiness. Suddenly, mysteriously, they were on the school stage. The whole school was clapping and cheering. Mrs. Bailey was up on the platform with them. She held up her hand. The cheering mob became still.

"It gives me great pleasure to announce the engagement between Jess Jordan and Gerard Play-Doh," she said. "May your babies be bilingual. I am going to sing a song of congratulation in a minute, but first I just have to take a dump." And she hitched her skirt up *right there on the platform*.

It was at this point that Jess realized it was all a dream. On the one hand, it was wonderful being with Gerard. On the other hand, she certainly didn't want to spend a second more with Mrs. Bailey. Jess knew how to wake herself up from bad dreams—she sort of stretched her eyes. But she didn't want to lose Gerard. Maybe she could suggest to Gerard that they fly right out of the window to a tropical island paradise. She turned to him. He was still holding her hand. But he had turned into a baboon.

"Agh!" cried Jess, waking up. For a moment she didn't recognize the curtains, and thought it was another dream. Then she remembered she'd spent the night in Mum's room. The bed was empty.

"Wake up, Jess!" Mum yelled up the stairs. "Everybody else is having their breakfast!"

"Coming!" shouted Jess, and crawled out of bed. Thank

goodness Mum had remembered to bring her school uniform up here, and clean undies and shirt. Otherwise she'd have had to go downstairs in her Winnie the Pooh pajamas. Almost worse than the dream, somehow.

As Jess joined the others for breakfast, the strange nightmarish atmosphere was still hanging around. Granny smiled at her, but it was a fairly feeble smile. She was clearly still sulking hard at Mum. Mum hadn't quite got rid of her headache and was taking some more pills. Edouard looked up briefly, nodded, said, "Good merning!" and buried his nose back in his hot chocolate.

"Good morning, Edouard! Good morning, everybody!" cried Jess, with pantomime panache. She'd almost never said "good morning" in her own home before. They'd been spared all that formal stuff up till now.

Edouard finished his bread, and Mum said something to him in French. He said, "Eskoos me," and went upstairs.

"He's gone to get his stuff," said Mum, who was finishing his packed lunch. "We need to leave in five minutes, Jess."

"Fine, OK," said Jess. "Make sure you put some chocolate biscuits in his lunchbox."

"I already have," said Mum rather snappishly. "I'm just going to the loo. Hurry up, Jess." There was the terrible sound of Edouard going into the bathroom upstairs. Everybody looked at the ceiling.

"Tough luck, Mum," said Jess. "You'll have to go in public like Mrs. Bailey in my dream last night."

"Thank God for the outside loo," said Mum, and disappeared through the back door. Jess and Granny were now alone for a split second.

"Granny," said Jess. "What's all this about your friend Gina charging you twenty pounds every time you have a conversation?"

Granny grabbed Jess's hand, leant in close, looked around in a conspiratorial way, and whispered, "It's not a conversation with her, dear. She puts me in touch with Grandpa."

"What?" gasped Jess. "You mean, like a séance or something?"

"She's a medium," said Granny. "And she's absolutely super. She talks to Grandpa as if he's still in the room. And she's given me all these messages from him—about things only he and I could know about. In my view, dear, it's money well spent, and if your mum tries to keep me here against my will, I want you to help me to escape."

Granny winked roguishly, but Jess had a feeling that underneath her light tone, she was deadly serious. Jess was simply amazed. As she sat there, trying to work out whether Granny was crazy or not, Edouard upstairs in the bathroom and Mum in the outside loo flushed in almost perfect unison. Jess hoped that, somehow, she was still asleep and this was some kind of deranged nightmare.

✳ 18 ✳

Jesus

The main task was to get Edouard to school in time to catch the bus for the Oxford trip. It was raining. As they ran to the car, Edouard pulled a gloomy face at the sky, as if to suggest that it never rained in France.

"The Queen is sneering at our magnificent British rain!" said Jess, as she fastened her seat belt.

"Well, at least he's got two pairs of trousers," said Mum. Edouard was wearing jeans today, and Granny had had instructions to find and repair the other trousers while everybody was out. "Imagine how awful it would be if he only had one pair. He might get arrested for exposing his buttocks to All Souls."

105

"Who are All Souls?" said Jess. "They sound like a rock band."

"It's an Oxford college," said her mum. "One of my friends had lunch there a few years ago and found himself standing next to Nelson Mandela at the urinal."

"Wow!" breathed Jess. "Some comfort stop!"

Soon they were at school. A bus was parked outside the gates, surrounded by a chaos of umbrellas. Jess and Edouard joined the throng. Edouard ran off without a backwards look. Jess searched for Flora.

Suddenly Gerard appeared, looking vague and stylish. When he saw her, he grinned. Jess felt herself blush, remembering the dream. It was insane, but she almost felt as if Gerard knew about the dream—as if he might have had it, too.

"Hi, Jezz," said Gerard.

"Hi, Gerard," said Jess. She could see Jodie fighting her way through the crowd towards them, looking jealous. "Enjoy Oxford," she said. "Hope your day is not too bof."

Gerard laughed. "Fanny!" he said. Jess gave a parting nod and slipped away. She wished he would stop that *fanny* business.

After registration, Jodie grabbed Jess and Flora. She looked round furtively as if she was about to reveal a big secret.

"It's on!" she whispered. "But my auntie says there can only be six of us! So it's going to be us three with Gerard, Edouard, and Marie-Louise. There's this amazing field just below her house, and there's a fantastic stream running along the bottom of it, and she's even got an outside loo, so we won't have to go indoors."

Jess was glad to hear about the outside loo. On a picnic, once, she had retreated into a small wood, and had an awful moment involving a nettle.

"My dad says this rain is just a front going through or something," said Flora. "There's still going to be a mini–heat wave at the weekend."

At this point the bell rang for home economics, and Jess realized that she would be required to make a pizza, and that she had forgotten the ingredients. That was the unfair thing about cooking. In all the other subjects, she could kind of busk and blag her way through. But not even Jess could make a pizza out of half a pack of chewing gum—though, if Jesus ever came back to earth, it might be just the sort of project he'd enjoy.

Jess noticed that if she added just one "u" to her name, it'd be Jesus. For a while she had wondered if it was a sign she was possibly the daughter of God, but she abandoned the idea after realizing that if God did intend to send a daughter this time, he wouldn't have chosen her mum as the surrogate mother. Jess's mum often swore and sometimes her fingernails were downright black. No, Jess was more likely to be the spawn of the devil than the Second Coming.

Comforted by this glamorous thought, Jess managed to get through home economics by shamelessly charming Mrs. Ford and confiding details of her mum's mercy dash to Granny's last night, and the fear that Granny was being exploited by a ruthless and charismatic predator. Mrs. Ford, who loved sensational confidences, forgave Jess for forgetting her ingredients and found some flour and cheese for her in her store cupboard.

"You should be a defense attorney when you leave school," said Flora. "You can wriggle out of anything."

Lunch seemed more relaxed without the French students, and the rain had stopped, so Jess, Flora, and Jodie took their baguettes to their favorite bench in the science quad. Two girls were sitting there. They were in the same year, but a different tutor group. Jess knew them by sight, but they had never talked. One was dark-haired and slightly spotty; the other was skinny, with ginger hair and a brace.

"Hey! This is our bench!" said Jodie. "Shift yo' asses, losers!"

"And we mean that in the nicest possible way," added Jess.

"It's OK, leave it. We can go to the field," said Flora.

"The field's wet," said Jodie. "We always sit here. It is *so* famously our spot." The ginger-haired girl flushed red with anger so that, for a moment, her freckles disappeared. Her green eyes sparkled.

"We were here first," she said.

"Don't pick a fight, Chloe," said the spotty girl. She turned to Jess. "You can sit here if you like. We were just going, anyway. That assembly you did last term was amazing."

"It was in the worst possible taste, though," said Jess, charmed that this person should have enjoyed her recent performance.

"Yeah, that's what I liked about it," said the girl. "All those thin people in Manhattan. 'Fifty pounds will keep a New York broker in cocktails for half an hour—please give generously.'" She laughed and got up.

"What's your name?" asked Jess, amazed that her tawdry

jests had, it seemed, been memorized. The red-haired friend was still sitting on the bench, and still glaring.

"I'm Zoe," said the spotty girl. "And this is Chloe."

"You should both marry the son of David Bowie," said Jess. She wished it could have been a better joke, but her fan laughed anyway.

"Come on, Chloe," said Zoe. "Let's go."

"Eat my shorts!" said Chloe, getting up and scorching past with a glare. She marched off. Zoe watched her go.

"She's a bit touchy today," she sighed. "She had a bit of a tragedy last night with one of her poison toads." Zoe shrugged apologetically and walked off.

"My God, I'm exhausted," said Jess, sitting down. "What does one have to do around here to get some respect?"

"How much respect do you want?" sneered Jodie, plonking herself down beside her. "She'll probably come back here when we've gone and sit down where you sat. It'll be a sacred spot."

"I had a crush once," said Flora. "On Miss Gregory. And I sat down where she'd been sitting on a bench in the gym, and it was still warm. I nearly fainted with delight."

Miss Gregory was a sports teacher. She was tall, dark, and handsome, with a slight mustache.

"Don't remind us," said Jess. "You'll put me off my lunch. I just hope Edouard hasn't got a crush on me after all. He shows no signs of it, anyway, thank God."

Suddenly a shadow fell across the bench. Fred had arrived. He seemed taller than ever, standing there against the sun, but somehow still not sinister, only absurd.

"So is the camping trip on?" he asked. "My dad says we

can have his old army tent. Just ignore the bullet holes and bloodstains."

"Sorry, Fred," said Jodie, in her brisk and rather brutal way, "you can't come. My auntie says we've got to keep the numbers down and six is the max."

"God, what a relief," said Fred. "I was heroically going to go through with it, but to be honest I'm allergic to being outdoors. In fact, I've had enough of this so-called fresh air. Ah well . . . I'm off to weep with disappointment in the loos." He strolled off.

"That was a bit harsh," said Jess. "Can't your auntie just let Fred come? Go on, let him. He's a laugh."

"Nope," said Jodie, biting through her chicken tikka baguette with an almost crocodile-like snap. "Six is the max."

"I feel sorry for him," said Flora. "He was so sweet offering his dad's tent and stuff."

"His tent sounded mank," said Jodie. "What's yours like? State of the art?"

Flora looked startled.

"We don't have a tent, actually," she said. "My mum refuses to stay in anything less than a four-star hotel."

"Have you got a tent, Jess?" asked Jodie.

"No," said Jess. "We sold ours years ago. But buy me the wool and I'll knit one by Friday." Despite the joke, she was feeling uneasy. Surely the weekend wasn't going to be scuppered by a lack of tents, for goodness' sake? "I kind of assumed you'd be providing the tents," she went on.

Jodie scowled. "Look, I'm providing the field, aren't I? Plus, unlike you two losers, I do actually have a tent, but it's way too small for all of us."

"I expect we can borrow one from somebody," said Flora. "Whizzer has a tent."

"He'd want something sordid in return," said Jodie. "We can borrow Fred's."

"What?" gasped Jess. "You can't tell him he can't come and then ask to borrow his tent. Have you no tact at all?"

The bell rang, bringing an end to their lunchtime idyll. A sense of uneasiness was creeping over them. Would their wonderful camping weekend have to be abandoned by a stupid thing like a shortage of tents? But then again, how could one go camping without them?

However, when Jess got home, she discovered that something much more fundamental was threatening her divine plans.

"Camping?" snapped her mum, struggling with a cheese sauce. (Jess had once again mistimed a crucial request.) "At this time of year? Forget it. We don't have a tent. It'll be too cold—he'll get pneumonia."

Edouard was sitting with Granny. He was pale with the awful aftermath of a trip to Oxford, and preparing to toy disgustedly with Mum's leeks and bacon in cheese sauce.

It's so infuriating, thought Jess. *Mum hates cooking with a ferocious passion and still she doesn't want to get him out of her hair for a weekend.*

Jess felt her heart sink down, down, down through the kitchen floor, the concrete foundations, and the coldest of cold clay, until it came to a dark, dripping cavern where vampire bats roosted. Here it came to rest. The camping trip was a nonstarter. This was a total, complete, and utter disaster.

✳ 19 ✳

fter supper Edouard scampered upstairs, muttering something about "'omework." Jess grabbed her mobile and texted Flora. **HELP! MUM SAYS NO TO CAMPING! GRIEF-STRICKEN! THINK OF SOMETHING!**

She approached her mum in the kitchen while she was loading the dishwasher. Jess knew this was not a good moment. First she had to ingratiate herself by chores. Jess put the salt and pepper away in the cupboard. She wiped down the work surfaces. She washed the baking tray—by hand, and then even dried the thing and put it away instead of just "leaving it to drain"—her usual cop-out. OK, she'd been saintly. Now she just had to let rip.

"Mum!" she burst out recklessly. "You have to change your mind. This camping trip is going to be the *best* time. Plus it gets Edouard out of your hair for a whole weekend. Me too, of course. I promise I'll look after him. If it rains for even a split second, we can go into Jodie's auntie's house."

Mum stood up and, as she did so, catastrophically banged her head on the cupboard door, which Jess had left open. She then staggered round the kitchen rubbing it and swearing so horribly that if she'd been a football player, she'd have been shown the red card and told to leave the field. Jess tried to fuss over her and console her and massage her head, but this kind concern only seemed to inflame Mum more. Jess did the only thing possible. She ran away.

Granny was in the sitting room, watching the TV news. Jess dived down beside her on the sofa and snuggled up close.

"A headless corpse has been found in the Thames," said Granny gleefully. "And strangely, it was wearing fancy dress." She was such a homicide addict.

"What kind of fancy dress?" asked Jess, desperate for distraction.

"It was a man wearing a 1940s cocktail frock," said Granny.

"Hmmmm," said Jess. "Might not have been fancy dress exactly. Might have been a tranny."

"A what, dear?" asked Granny. "Did you say 'granny'?" She looked alarmed.

"No, Granny, nothing," whispered Jess, and patted her hand reassuringly. Granny hadn't completely got the hang of cross-dressing yet, let alone sex-change operations. It was a long, slow, tactful process, educating your grandparent in the ways of the modern world.

Mum stuck her head round the sitting room door and announced that she was going up to her study to do some paperwork. She ordered Jess to do her homework or there would be big trouble.

"I promise I'll start in five minutes!" said Jess, and snuggled up closer to Granny. The news had moved on to less exciting topics—something to do with taxes.

"So what's the matter, dear?" whispered Granny, once Mum had gone. Swiftly Jess outlined the fabulous camping plan, and Mum's hostile reaction to it.

"I can understand you all wanting to be together in a big field," said Granny. "It sounds lovely. Why don't you ring your father and see if he can put in a good word for you?"

"Granny, you're a genius!" said Jess, kissing the old dear vigorously on the cheek. "But first—how are things with you? Are you still under house arrest?"

"Something marvelous happened today, dear," said Granny, leaning in close. "While I was mending Edouard's trousers."

"What? What?" gasped Jess.

"I heard Grandpa speak to me," hissed Granny. "I heard his voice out loud, right in the room, as if he was sitting in that chair." Goose bumps zipped up and down Jess's back.

"What did he say?" breathed Jess.

"He said, 'You don't need that Gina, sweetheart. You can talk to me anytime you want.'" As a message from the Beyond, this was both reassuring and economical. "Don't tell your mum, though," Granny went on, "because she'll think I'm losing my marbles. I'm just going to say that I've seen sense, and I promise not to have any more readings with Gina. And you must back me up, dear."

"Of course, Granny! And you back me up about the camping."

Granny sighed and shook her head. "I don't think she'll take any notice of what I say, dear," she said. "I'll do my best, though."

"OK—I'm going to phone Dad right now," said Jess. She ran to the kitchen and picked up the phone. Thank goodness Mum was not talking to anybody from her study upstairs. Jess had to use the landline, but it wasn't always completely private. She'd promised never to phone her dad from her mobile except in emergencies. Although this was an emergency, in a way. She dialed. He answered. Jess let him have the whole drama, down to the last tent peg.

"So you've got to persuade Mum to say yes!" pleaded Jess. "Everybody else is going, and it'll be dire if Edouard and I are stuck here together on our own all weekend. He just, like, totally can't speak English and I can't speak French. He's only happy when he's got his French friends around."

"I see the problem," said Dad. "But does it have to be camping?"

"Yes, it does have to be camping!" said Jess. "It'll be wonderful! Granny thinks it'll be lovely!"

"What if it rains?"

"The weather forecast says there's going to be a mini–heat wave! Flora's dad says so and he's never wrong."

"What are the sleeping arrangements? How many tents are there?"

"For God's sake, Dad! You're supposed to be my groovy, artistic, easygoing parent, who cheerfully says yes to all my delightful plans!"

"Sorry," said Dad. "But I am concerned . . . You know, I don't want to tread on Mum's toes . . . and I share her worries about your safety."

"Safety!" exploded Jess. "We'll practically be in Jodie's auntie's garden! What could happen?"

"Don't ask me to speculate!" said Dad, sounding nervous. "My blood runs cold at the thousands of terrible things that could happen."

"You wimp!" said Jess. "I was going to ask you to plead with Mum on my behalf, but don't bother." She was really angry with her dad now. "How's everything going for your exhibition? OK?" But she said it in a really cross, sarcastic voice.

"Never mind the exhibition," said Dad. "We were talking about this camping trip. To be honest, even if I did think it was a good idea, I don't think I'd have any influence on Mum. In fact, asking me to back you up might be the worst move you could make. What sort of mood is she in?"

"She's just banged her head on the cupboard door," said Jess. "Plus Edouard left most of his leek and bacon in cheese sauce. And Granny is going through a slightly crazy patch—hearing the voices of the dead, that sort of thing."

"Right," said Dad. "Not only is it a bad thing in general, getting me to ask Mum to let you do something, but at this moment in particular I'd say it was sheer lunacy for anyone to say anything to her, except possibly, 'Mum, would you like me to bring you a cup of tea?'"

"OK, never mind." Jess felt herself plummeting down into doom again. "It's obvious you can't help. Talk to you again soon. Bye." She put the phone down without even waiting for Dad to say "Love you," as he usually did. And she hadn't said "Love you" herself, either. She felt slightly sick about that. But she was furious that Dad wouldn't back her up. He was so spineless sometimes—especially when it came to talking to Mum.

Jess went downstairs into her room and sat glumly at her desk. The photo of Edouard was still pinned to her notice-board. His smile didn't look glamorous anymore, now she knew he was barely five feet tall. She couldn't believe she'd thought he looked a bit like Orlando Bloom. She ripped it off the board and threw it in the bin. Then she suddenly thought that, if by some preposterous accident Edouard might come into her room, he might see his photo in her rubbish bin and feel hurt. So she picked it up and put it out of sight in a drawer.

Her mobile buzzed. There was a text from Flora: **WORK-ING ON IT. GIVE ME TIME.** Jess instantly texted back. **I BEG YOU, FIX IT AND I WILL WORSHIP YOU ALWAYS.**

Amid the deep, desolate, echoing despair there was the faintest hint of hope.

✳ 20 ✳

*J*ess got out her homework books. They weighed a ton. How ironical it was that her granny could continue to talk to her grandpa even after he'd been dead for months, but her stupid parents couldn't exchange a few words on the phone even though they were still alive. Especially as whenever her mum talked to anybody about the divorce, she always smiled in a superior kind of way and said, "It's all very amicable."

If this is amicable, thought Jess, *don't let me ever have to experience hostile*. She did some homework. It felt almost soothing, it was so far removed from her present traumas. Jess had to draw a map of the world and shade in the area covered by coniferous forests. For a brief half hour she imagined a carefree life spent frolicking in the forests with Flora and Fred, but eventually she realized that the frolicking would probably be forbidden by feeble parents worried about fierce, ferocious, fanged wolves, bears, and other feral fauna.

The phone rang. Jess's heart leapt, and she jumped up, but she was only halfway to the door when her mum answered it, upstairs in her study. There was a moment's pause, and then she called, "Jess! It's Dad!"

Jess ran out to the kitchen, grabbed the phone, and said, "Hello!" She heard the faint click of her mum replacing the phone upstairs.

"You hung up on me," said Dad.

"Sorry," said Jess. "I was in a total strop. I do love you, though. Honest."

"I do love you, too," said Dad. "And I've had a think about it and I'll talk to Mum about the camping trip if you like."

"But, Dad—you spoke to her just now."

"Yes, but I thought I'd better talk to you first and see if anything else had happened since we spoke. Any more developments to the melodrama?"

"No. I'll get her now. Hang on!"

Jess raced upstairs, only to see her mum disappearing into the bathroom.

"Mum! Wait!" she called. "Dad wants to speak to you!"

Her mum didn't even pause. She just kind of flared her eyes slightly as she closed the bathroom door in Jess's face.

"I'm having a bath now!" she said through the door.

"Apologize to him for me! We can catch up later on." Jess heard the bath taps being turned on.

Jess's heart sank yet again. She went into Mum's study and picked up the phone there.

"Sorry, Dad," she said. "Mum's in the loo, and she's running a bath, and she's already getting undressed, and she can't come out because of Edouard." She felt she had to exaggerate her mum's situation so Dad wouldn't be offended. She seemed to spend so much of her time as a kind of diplomatic go-between, when her parents, being technically adults, should have been able to communicate politely themselves.

"Oh well." Dad sounded relieved that he didn't have to speak to Mum. He just couldn't hide it. "Never mind. Maybe later. Or tomorrow."

"You're such a wuss," said Jess. "I can see you wriggling out of it. By tomorrow it'll be too late. Ring in about an hour, OK?"

"OK," said Dad doubtfully. "I'll try."

"*Try?!?*" snapped Jess. "You pick the phone up, dial, and speak. What's so difficult?"

"Sorry," said Dad. "I admit, I am hopeless." But even the way he said it was kind of satisfied. Jess felt irritated, but she decided she simply had to keep her temper now, and say goodbye in a civilized way.

Suddenly she heard Edouard's door open. He went downstairs—normally, this time.

"OK, Dad," she said. "The French boy's just gone downstairs. I ought to go and be with Granny. She speaks even less French than I do, which is totally nil."

Dad said goodbye, and Jess paid a fleeting visit to Mum's bedroom mirror, shuddered in dismay, and went downstairs. She had assumed that Granny would be watching TV and Edouard would be standing about awkwardly, but to her surprise they were both sitting at the kitchen table, and Granny had got out her packs of cards and was shuffling them.

"Ah, hello, dear," she said. "We were going to play bezique, but we can play belote instead if you want to join us, because bezique's just for two." Jess was amazed. Her granny's packs of cards had been a constant part of Jess's childhood, but she hadn't realized that some of the games Granny played had French names. Edouard was looking relaxed for once.

"Yes, why not?" said Jess. "And afterwards maybe we can play poker for matchsticks."

Half an hour later, Jess realized she was beginning to feel a lot better. Edouard had smiled a few times. Granny seemed to have melted him, the old charmer that she was. He had won most of the card games. They were planning a hot chocolate and chocolate biscuit break in five minutes, which would surely transform him into a purring pussycat.

Then the phone rang. Jess jumped up to answer it, half expecting it would be Dad again. But it wasn't.

"Hello," said a woman's voice. "Could I speak to Mrs. Jordan, please? This is Rose Bradshaw." The woman sounded quite posh but sort of shy and dreamy.

"Oh yes, of course. Hang on a minute, I'll go and find her," said Jess, slightly intimidated. She ran upstairs and knocked on the bathroom door. Mum was having one of her endless soaky baths.

"Mum!" she called. "There's a phone call for you! A strange woman! She sounds important! Her name's Rose Bradshaw!"

"Rose Bradshaw?" said Mum, sounding startled.

"Maybe it's somebody from the library!" said Jess. "Come quick!"

"I don't know that name at all. Tell her I'll be there in a minute," said Mum, sounding flustered. Jess could hear splashy sounds of her getting out of the bath.

Typical, thought Jess. *When an unknown woman rings, Mum scrambles out of the bath in ludicrous haste: when my actual dad rings, her literal ex and only husband, she locks herself in the bathroom even though she hasn't even started undressing.*

"Don't tell her I was in the bath!" added Mum, sounding foolishly guilty for some reason.

"Why not?" asked Jess. "It's not illegal."

"If you say I was in the bath she'll feel guilty she rang so late," said Mum. "Oh, don't bother—I'm nearly ready. . . ." And then suddenly the bathroom door was flung open and Mum, swathed in towels, rushed past into her study. "Don't worry, I'll deal with it," she added, and picked up the phone.

"Hello?" she said. Jess loitered on the landing, eavesdropping. "Yes . . . Yes. Ah, I see . . . Jess!" called her mum. "Please could you go downstairs and put the phone down? I can hear Granny talking down there."

Jess went downstairs. Granny was making the hot chocolate and merrily telling Edouard about her arthritic hip. He couldn't have understood a word, but he didn't seem to mind. Granny had found the chocolate biscuits and he was getting stuck in. Jess replaced the phone.

A few minutes later, Mum came downstairs in her naff old jog pants and fleece.

"That was Jodie's aunt," she said. "She had a long talk with me and reassured me that this camping trip is going to be properly organized. Apparently Fred's providing a big tent for the boys and Mrs. Bradshaw's providing a big tent for the girls, and she's going to keep an eye on you all, and if it rains you can all move to the barn."

"So it's OK, then?" Jess hardly dared breathe.

"I suppose so," said Mum, with just a hint of reluctant sulkiness.

"Brilliant!" said Jess.

Later that evening, after a lot more card games, Jess had a call from Flora, who explained how it had all happened.

"My mum rang Jodie's mum and got Jodie's auntie's number," she said. "And my mum talked to her. And then Jodie's mum rang a friend of hers who has an amazing tent. And then I rang Jodie and persuaded her to let Fred come. And then Mum rang Fred's mum, and, and then . . . oh, there were loads more phone calls with the grown-ups all faffing around and fussing about details, and eventually they got it all sorted."

"You beauty!" said Jess. "A gold star for fixing! Tomorrow I shall kiss your feet—no, wait, your hand—no, sorry— well, I'll refrain from punching you. Will that do?"

"Oh yes, that's such a relief!" said Flora. "Anyway, I hope this camping trip lives up to the promise. I mean, after everything we've been through to get it sorted, it'd be terrible if it was a disaster, wouldn't it?"

"What can go wrong?" said Jess confidently. She just knew it was going to be brilliant.

As she kissed Granny good night later, Granny gave the thumbs-up.

"So pleased your camping trip is on after all!" she whispered. They were in Jess's room, where Granny was going to sleep, but Mum could just have overheard. "I expect it was Grandpa's influence!" And Granny gave a ludicrous wink. Jess didn't have the heart to tell her that no, it had been Flora and Flora's mum.

But then, who knows? Maybe Grandpa had sent down some positive vibes. Jess did hope that Granny would cut down on the supernatural stuff soon, though. It was just a tad creepy and weird.

*T*he field was divine. The sun was shining. It was gloriously warm for so early in the year, and Marie-Louise was already showing a convenient appetite for chores. She was unpacking all the catering stuff and arranging it tidily on a couple of boxes, near where they planned to have the campfire. Jodie's uncle had brought them a load of dry wood. Jess was looking forward to sitting round the campfire and possibly singing silly songs tonight, under the stars.

The girls' tent was a fabulous modern one that had kind of leapt into shape all by itself, enabling Flora, Jodie, and Jess to sit on a blanket and jeer while they watched the boys struggling with Fred's father's old army tent. It didn't really have any bloodstains and bullet holes, but there were loads of guy ropes and poles and things and the whole thing kept sagging in the middle.

"It's a good job Gerard's so tall," sighed Jodie, proudly watching as her dreamboat held up one end of the tent. Gerard was wearing a vest-type T-shirt that revealed his olive skin. Occasionally he looked over to the girls, grinned and shrugged in a cool kind of way, but nobody could tell who he was grinning at because, of course, he was wearing his shades.

"On the other hand, it's a disaster that Fred's so tall," said Jess. Fred was fussing with the other side of the tent and tripping over the tent pegs.

"It's a shame Edouard is such an insane little dork," said Jodie. "Never mind, Jess, maybe it'll be your turn next year."

This was Jodie's way of warning Jess and Flora that Gerard was, in some territorial kind of way, utterly hers. Even though everybody had noticed Gerard's tendency to escape from Jodie's side whenever possible and chat to other girls.

"Don't forget that Fred and I are practically married," said Jess with a broad wink, in case Marie-Louise overheard. Although Edouard hadn't been so gross as to reveal a sordid passion for her, she didn't want to encourage him by appearing available. "And anyway, I absolutely adore Edouard. I've taught him to beg for biscuits and I'm having him wormed and de-flea'd next week." Flora giggled uncontrollably. Her laugh was infectious, like a rippling stream that just went on and on.

Edouard was floundering about somewhere inside the boys' tent, trying to hold the thing up from the inside. He appeared to be enjoying himself in a grim kind of way. He was interested in nature and had already found some really sexy beetles by the stump of a dead old tree. He hadn't even looked at Jess for hours. It was wonderful.

"Oh, this place!" drooled Flora, shaking her golden locks in the dazzling sunshine. "It's absolute heaven! Look at that lovely stream down there. I'm going to sunbathe. I'll have to send my dad a text promising him I'm wearing factor thirty, though."

Jess decided she would text her dad, too, even though he hadn't rung back on the night of the Permission to Camp crisis. He'd texted her much, much later that night. **SORRY FORGOT TO RING AND NOW TOO LATE. USELESS. SORRY. SORRY SORRY. SHOOT ME—IT'D BE KINDEST IN THE LONG RUN. USELESS DAD. XXXX**

"I'm going to go and paddle in the stream," said Flora, getting up. "Anybody want to come?"

"*Somebody's* going to get the fire going," said Jodie in a martyred kind of way. "And cook the supper."

"Marie-Louise loves cooking," said Flora. "And she's already unpacked all the stuff."

"So stop moaning, Jodie!" said Jess. "Maybe Gerard can help you to get the fire going." The boys' tent was nearly sorted. "Once we've had our paddle we'll come back and help with the grub."

Jess linked arms with Flora and they strolled off down the slope to the stream. It was already slightly tricky when Jodie was around. She had a tendency to attach herself to them, and then try and boss them about, while permitting them no quality time alone to bitch and giggle.

"Gerard could probably kindle fire just by giving the twigs a smoldering look," Jess whispered into Flora's ear. "God, he's so up himself!"

"He is slightly gorgeous, though," said Flora.

"Hmmm," said Jess. She didn't want to admit she'd already had an exciting dream about Gerard. Well, exciting apart from that bit at the end where he had turned into a baboon. "I suppose he's OK if you like that sort of thing. And personally, of course, I *do*. I don't know what's the matter with me at the moment. I fancy everybody."

"Me too," said Flora. "I even fancied a traffic warden yesterday."

"I even fancy dead traffic wardens," said Jess.

"I even fancy dead, gay traffic wardens," said Flora.

"I hope there's nothing too revolting in that water," pondered Jess as they arrived at the stream. "Or I might just have to fancy it."

They sat down and took their shoes and socks off. The stream was rushing along, making a fabulous splashy gurgling sort of sound—a bit like Flora laughing, of course. There was a rope hanging from a tree—evidently kids had been down here playing at Tarzan and swinging across.

"Right, then," said Jess. "Off you go. You're the team leader, obviously, and you have to inspire your team by wading in bravely." Jess was secretly planning to stay on the bank if Flora's scream as she entered the cold water was too piercingly loud.

"How deep do you think it is?" said Flora warily, getting to her feet and wriggling her toes.

"Hardly up to your ankles," said Jess. "You can see the bottom, for God's sake, Flo. Wait! Maybe you should send a text to your dad. 'Am paddling in stream, Dad, but relax, it's only six inches deep.'"

Flora picked her way gingerly to the water's edge and hesitated for about three hours.

"Stand on that big brown stone," suggested Jess. "But be gentle with it, because I'm starting to fancy it, in the absence of any male animals."

Flora extended her beautiful foot and trod on the stone. It rocked treacherously, jolting her off-balance. She staggered about in the stream, splashing and screaming with laughter, and somehow managed to avoid falling over. "It's absolutely freezing!" she yelled. "I'm coming out!"

"Well done, though," said Jess. "You could win a gold medal at Paddling for England."

Flora lurched out and landed on the grass. Her feet were muddy and kind of mottled with shock, but they were still, of course, the most beautiful feet for miles. "We should have brought a towel," said Flora. "I'll have to go back to the tent. Coming?"

"I don't know . . . ," said Jess. "I think I'm just going to text my dad. I'll come up in a minute." Flora went off, and Jess got out her phone.

AM SITTING BESIDE STREAM IN WHAT I BELIEVE IS CALLED "NATURE." HOPE YOU'RE IMPRESSED. ALL WELL. BOYS SHARING TENT, GIRLS SHARING DIFFERENT TENT. NO DRUGS, NO ALCOHOL. ONLY THREAT TO HEALTH UNDERCOOKED SAUSAGES. HOPE EXHIBITION GOES WELL. LOVE, JESS.

She whizzed off the text and then sat and stared at the stream for a while. Then her phone buzzed in reply.

WISH I WAS THERE ALTHOUGH I DO REALIZE THAT WOULD BE DISASTROUS FOR YOU. HAVE FUN. PRIVATE VIEW STARTS IN 2 HRS. MUST GO AND SUGAR MY HAIR. LOVE DAD XX

Jess smiled. She just *had* to go down to Cornwall and see Dad this summer. She'd never even visited his new house down there. He often came up to town and they'd had a million laughs and done lots of crazy things, and seen movies and gone skating and had pizzas and stuff, but Jess really wanted to see where he lived, so she could imagine him just chilling out at home. She sighed.

Suddenly she heard footsteps and the chink of bottles. She turned round and there was Gerard, sauntering down towards her and carrying an armful of lemonade, Red Bull, and Coke.

"Hi, Jezz!" he said. Behind him, up at the top end of the field, Jess could see smoke—the campfire had evidently got going. Gerard carefully put the bottles on the grass and sat down beside her.

"Jodie h'asked me to cool zese bottles," he said. "In ze stream." He lifted his shades up off his eyes and parked them on top of his head.

God, his eyes were amazing. A sort of wonderful green with little flecks of gold in them. Jess stared at Gerard, and, rather amazingly, Gerard stared right back. And very much against her will, Jess felt that the campfire was not the only thing starting to smolder and fizz. Now that Gerard had arrived, she didn't have to fancy that boring old stone anymore. Here was a much more promising object.

✳ 22 ✳

Je t'aime

"Right . . . ," said Jess. Suddenly her mind had gone blank.

"Say somesing fanny, Jezz," said Gerard in a soft, low, purring voice. "You are h'amusing."

Jess blushed. Gerard's divine eyes were kind of melting her soul, to put it mildly. How could she think of anything fanny to say at a time like this?

She rolled over onto her tummy and picked up a bottle, then crawled to the water's edge.

"We can stick them in the mud so they don't get carried off downstream," she said. As witty remarks go, it wasn't prizewinning, but it was at least words in a row that made sense. Considering how fast Jess's heart was beating, this was quite an achievement.

Gerard wriggled up beside her and they placed all the bottles in the stream. The silence was kind of ominous. They were lying so close together, their arms were almost touching. Their hands were in the water. Gerard scooped up a handful of mud.

"How you say?" he asked.

"Mud," said Jess. Then she realized it sounded like the one word of French everybody knows: *merde*. Meaning, of course, poo. "Mud," she repeated. "Not *merde*."

Gerard laughed. "You are fanny!" he said.

"Er—funny, not fanny," said Jess. "Fuh-nee."

"You are fuh-nee!" repeated Gerard, grinning sideways at her.

"What's the French for *mud*?" asked Jess. Not that she cared. It was just that every time Gerard looked at her, a kind of firework show went off inside her, and normal conversation was impossible, so she might as well learn a bit of French.

"Ze mud—*la boue*," said Gerard.

"What?—Boo?" asked Jess. What a weird language French was. So if you hid behind a door, then jumped out and said "Boo!" in French, you'd be saying "Mud!"

"*Oui, la boue*," said Gerard, staring deeply into her eyes. "I ham your French teacher."

"You sure are, sweetie!" cried Jess, unable to contain a surge of delight. She scooped up a handful of mud. "And *boue* to you!" she added playfully, and slapped the mud all over his hand. She was flirting for England, and on line for the gold medal.

"And *boue* to you, too!" said Gerard, laughing, and he scooped and slopped a handful right back onto her hands. God, this was exciting. Jess could suddenly understand the charm of mud-wrestling. Just as long as she could do it with Gerard.

Suddenly Gerard grabbed her hand, underwater. He pretended he was washing the mud off. A few crazy rockets went off in Jess's chest. Gerard started playing with her fingers underwater, and then basically squeezed her hand, hard, and wouldn't let her go. He peeped sideways at her with a sexy grin. Jess felt delightfully sick. And amazed. Could this really be happening? Could a guy she fancied actually be holding her hand? But there was a snake in this paradise.

"What about Jodie?" whispered Jess. Jodie was miles away at the top of the field, but still Jess could almost feel her watching.

Gerard shrugged—even though he was lying down. An English guy would never be able to do something like that. These Latin lovers were so supple.

"Jodie is my 'ostess," he said. "She is not my gairlfriend. But—what about Fred?"

"Oh, Fred!" Jess's heart gave a dangerous lurch. "Fred and I . . ." her mind raced. What could she say? She didn't want to admit all that stuff about pretending to be Fred's girlfriend to put Edouard off. It seemed a bit anti-French. Besides, it was quite difficult to explain even in English.

"Fred and I are finished," she said. "We had a big row."

Gerard's eyebrows went up quite a way. These Latin lovers had different facial expressions from English boys. Their faces were like a ballet, honestly. And what wonderful eyebrows Gerard had! Jess could never get hers to look half as good, even after two hours' plucking.

"You and Fred are finished?" he asked. "But you still are ze friends?"

"Oh yes—just good friends now," said Jess hastily.

Gerard looked puzzled. Maybe the French didn't do amicable. Maybe when they split up they always had a raging row and then threw themselves off a bridge into the River Seine. They were so tempestuous. It was marvelous.

"Gerard!" Oh God. It was Jodie's voice, and she was bearing down on them like a Panzer tank. Instantly Gerard let go of Jess's hand, even though they had been holding hands invisibly, underwater. Jess felt guilty, too. "How's the drink coming along?" Jodie plonked herself down between them.

"Nice and cold," said Jess, getting to her feet. She just couldn't bear to stay another minute, now Jodie had arrived to wreck the atmosphere. She might just have to hit her, and as Jodie's aunt was providing the field, it would seem ungrateful.

"I'm going to sort my stuff out," said Jess. She set off up the field. Her hands were still wet and tingling—tingling with the ice-cold water and the memory of Gerard's sexy French fingers. She had held hands with a dreamboat! But did it still count if it had been underwater?

The campfire was blazing nicely, and normally it would have looked kind of inviting, with Marie-Louise frying sausages, Edouard playing with his new pet beetle, and Flora staring romantically into the flames. But part of Jess was still down by the stream, holding hands underwater with Gerard. So much had happened in just a few minutes. The world had changed utterly.

"Did you text your dad?" asked Flora. For a moment Jess blinked and stared. It seemed ages, even days, since she had texted her dad.

"Yeah—his private view starts in a couple of hours," said Jess, recovering.

"Oh, I hope it goes well for him," said Flora. "You'll be thinking about him."

"Mmm," said Jess. Thinking about Dad? No way. She was barely able to reply coherently to Flora. All she could think about was that Gerard and Jodie were coming back up the field. She could see them out of the corner of her eye. Oh my God! Her heart was starting to race again. Would she blush when he looked at her? Would she give herself away? She sat down next to Flora and fiddled with her shoe, so she wouldn't have to look up when Jodie and Gerard arrived.

"Give him my love," said Flora. For a moment Jess's brain just refused to comprehend. She stared blankly at Flora. Who? What? What was she saying? Was it anything to do with Gerard?

"What?"

"Give your dad my love and tell him I hope the exhibition goes brilliantly," said Flora. She was so polite, it almost hurt. "When you next text him or call him, I mean," she added, even more politely.

"OK, you morons!" Jodie had arrived, and now politeness

must die. "Shove up and make room for the King and Queen of the Camp!" Jess fixed her eyes firmly on the fire. She knew if she caught Gerard's eye now, she would faint.

"If it's camp you're after," said Fred, who was clambering out of the boys' tent, holding a book, "I'm your man. Give me some gold high-heeled shoes and I'll do my dizzy blonde at the premiere routine." He struck a camp pose and pouted. Everybody laughed. Marie-Louise turned to Jess with a sweet, sweet smile.

"Your Fred is so wonderful!" she said. Panic rose in Jess's throat. He couldn't be *her* Fred now: that would be a disaster. If everyone still thought she was with Fred, what were her chances of becoming an item with Gerard? She was dumbstruck. How did she get out of this?

"Ah, wife!" said Fred, in a stupid posh booming voice, pretending to be drunk. "Make room! I'm coming over! I wish to discuss the gas bill with you!" He crashed down beside her and, in an infuriating parody of affection, threw his arm around her shoulder. "It's our anniversary next week, you know," he said to Marie-Louise, who giggled. "What is it, wife? Not gold or silver—paper, maybe? Yes! I'll give you a designer bogroll to celebrate!"

"Get off, Fred!" snapped Jess, with real venom. This stupid act of Fred's couldn't have been worse timed. She was going to have to pick a fight with him right now. They were going to have to have an almighty bust-up in public. And as she was really annoyed with Fred, it was going to be convincing. She just hoped Fred would sort of understand, and go along with it. You never could tell with Fred.

✳23✳

*J*ess scrambled to her feet and turned on Fred, who
looked puzzled. She was horribly aware of Gerard
looking up at her. Jess knew her right profile was
her worst, and having a face contorted with fury didn't do
anything for a girl's sex appeal.

"Fred!" she snapped.

"What, wife?" Fred looked up in a comic parody of fear.
He was cringing for England. "What have I done now? Left
my dirty socks on the floor?"

"Stop calling me 'wife'!" shouted Jess. "It's so stupid! That
joke is so last century! Come over here! We've gotta talk!"

Jess ran over to a nearby tree, and Fred stumbled to his

feet and followed—shrugging to everybody as he left the fireside, as if Jess was in the grips of some madness. Which, of course, she was. Love madness.

"So?" Fred arrived under the tree. Its canopy gave them a little bit of privacy. "What next?"

"We have a flaming row and we split up," hissed Jess.

"Just like that? Just like that?" jabbered Fred. "How? How? What about?"

"Get on with it!" snapped Jess. "You're so goddamn brilliant in the drama lessons, just think of it as an improvisation."

"Wait! Wait! Why are we doing this?" asked Fred.

"I'll tell you later!"

"What's my motivation?"

"Oh, for God's sake, Fred!" roared Jess (a shout like that would sound convincing). "You've been seeing someone else."

"That's a lie!" shouted Fred. "It was you—you and that Norman!"

"Norman?" yelled Jess. "He's just my mum's gardener, OK? He's, like, forty years old! Plus he has body odor. That's just an insult! You can't wriggle out of this one, Fred Parsons. It's over, and it's been over ever since I found out about you and that tart Gloria!"

"I was just getting a smut out of her eye!" protested Fred. He was grinning now, enjoying himself.

"*Stop grinning, stop grinning, make it look real!*" whispered Jess, then out loud: "That is just such a lie! You're trash!"

"Trash?" Fred exploded. "You're the one who's trash! Anything in trousers!—Never mind Norman, what about

Cyril? And Hannibal? And Sam? And, and, and Adam? *Whoops,*" whispered Fred. *"Ran out of names there for a moment and had to go back to the Bible!"*

Jess was totally dismayed that Fred had made her sound like a slut. "Don't talk to me anymore!" she yelled, really angry. "I'm sick of your lies and inventions! OK? Let's leave it! We're ruining everybody's evening!"

Fred shrugged and shook his head.

Jess walked away and rejoined the others. She caught Flora's eye. Flora looked embarrassed, amused, and also dangerously near giggling. She, of course, knew it had all been a charade. It was the French people—Gerard in particular—who had to be convinced. Marie-Louise gave her a sympathetic look. She was nearly in tears.

"I am so sorry, Jess," she whispered, and grabbed Jess's arm. Jess tried hard to look tragic, and nodded.

"It's OK," she said. "I told Fred it was over after I found out he was seeing . . ." For a terrible moment she forgot the name of Fred's fictional squeeze.

"Gloria," prompted Flora.

"I can hardly bring myself to say her name without bursting into tears," said Jess, between clenched teeth.

"Awful! Awful!" said Marie-Louise, and stroked Jess's arm sympathetically. She was such a sweetheart.

"Anyway," said Jess, taking a deep breath and looking around at everybody except Gerard. "Now we've got that sorted, let's have some fun!"

"How about charades?" suggested Flora.

"You mean, *more* charades?" murmured Jess out of the side of her mouth.

"Come on, Fred!" called Flora. "Charades! You're the champion!" Fred came out from under the tree and marched up to the fireside.

"OK," he said, and offered his hand to Jess. "Divorced, then? You can keep the cat—I'll have the grand piano and the Ferrari."

Jess reached up and shook his hand. For once she couldn't think of anything to say. She just wanted to get the moment over, and was grateful to Fred for managing to make a joke of it.

"You go first, Fred," said Flora. She was really tactful and clever at times like this. She could smooth anybody's ruffled feelings. Even if they were all a bit of a charade in the first place.

"Let's do bands," said Jodie. The Frenchies all looked puzzled. Flora patted Marie-Louise on the hand.

"Don't worry," she said. "You'll soon understand it."

"OK," said Fred, gangling in his absurd way a few yards from the fire. He twanged on an imaginary guitar and shook his head like somebody possessed.

"OK, OK, it's a band!" yelled Jodie. "We knew that already! Get on with it."

Fred held up one finger. "One word!" yelled Jodie. She was so loud. Gerard had to sit next to her, and it must have been really hard for him to stay polite, what with her throwing herself at him. Jodie was so upfront and pushy all the time.

Fred launched into his charade. He staggered about, gasping, with his tongue hanging out. Everybody started laughing—even the French students. Fred could be just hilarious. He was a natural clown.

"Water! Water!" gasped Fred, sinking to his knees. "Perrier! Evian!—Ah!" he crawled along a few yards, his eyes huge with longing. Then he started to slurp from an imaginary pool. "I'd prefer Pepsi, obviously," he said in an aside, "but there's hardly any slime, so it'll have to do."

"Oasis!" cried Jess, in a flash of inspiration. Everybody cheered, and Fred collapsed down onto the grass, across the fire from Jess.

"Your turn, Jess!" said Jodie.

Jess got up, feeling awkward. She still hadn't dared to even take a peep at Gerard and now she had to perform a ridiculous charade in front of him. She decided to do Atomic Kitten. She dropped down to the ground and started meowing and scratching.

"Cat something!" said Flora.

"Pussy—somesing?" said Gerard. It was time to explode.

"*Brooooooooagh!*" yelled Jess, exploding in an atomic way all over the grass. Hardly her most elegant and seductive moment. She should have chosen something a little more dignified, dammit.

At this of all moments, somehow, she caught Gerard's eye. He was grinning at her and his eyes looked strangely shiny.

"Do eet again!" he said. Jodie shot him a sharp look.

"I know! It's Atomic Kitten!" said Flora, just in time. Jess was sure her second explosion would have been even worse. She might have spat in his eye, or something.

"I sink ze sausages are ready!" said Marie-Louise. The beans were also bubbling nicely.

"OK, suppertime!" announced Jodie. "We can do some more charades afterwards!"

She was really getting irritating. Jess sneaked another look at Gerard, and to her amazement he wasn't looking at the food, like everybody else. He was looking right at her, and his eyes were kind of smiley and magnetic. Suddenly Jess lost her appetite. Could this be love? As for Gerard, he was gazing at her as if she was some kind of delicious chocolate cake. As if he wanted to gobble her up.

What on earth was going to happen after supper? How were they going to get some time alone together? Jess was beginning to have a burning ambition—to be French kissed by a French boy.

24

*S*upper was great: jacket potatoes, beans, and sausages. The jacket spuds had been done in Jodie's auntie's oven, indoors, which was cheating, really, but who cared? It was all delish. Jess, however, was having problems eating. Despite a lifetime of rampant greed, she now struggled to force down a few mouthfuls. Once or twice she took a quick peep at Gerard.

The first time, he was eating his potato skin, whole, and had stuff hanging out of his mouth and a smear of ketchup on his face, but it only made Jess love him more. The second time she looked, she caught his eye, and for a split second there was a flash of electricity between them so powerful,

Jess was afraid her bra fastening might have melted and her earrings fused to her lobes.

Everybody carried the dirty dishes indoors to Jodie's auntie's kitchen for the washing-up. Mrs. Bradshaw herself was sitting in a little office beyond the kitchen, dealing with an enormous pile of paperwork.

"Take your shoes off!" she shouted whenever the back door opened. A smelly old sheepdog lay in a basket by the Aga and she wagged her tail lazily whenever anyone arrived, and gave a kind of grunt.

"This is Betsy," said Jodie. "She's retired."

"I won't bother to bark when I'm retired, either," said Jess.

The washing-up was all done by Marie-Louise and Edouard. Jodie had worked out a rota. Jodie was due to do the chores tomorrow lunchtime with—guess who? Gerard. It was kind of pathetic.

But Jess could understand why Jodie was so besotted with him. Whenever Jess heard his name or caught sight of him, her whole body kind of exploded secretly. It was so bizarre.

"So," said Jodie as they gathered round the fire again after all the chores were done. "Hmmmm, what now? I know! Sardines!"

"Sardines?" protested Jess feebly. "But we've just had supper!"

"No, it's a game," said Jodie. "We used to play it when I was a kid. One person goes off to hide, and the others all look for him. Or her."

"What, like hide-and-seek?" asked Flora.

"No, it's the opposite, really, because in hide-and-seek you all go and hide, but in Sardines only one person goes and the rest look for him, and if you find him, you join him and hide with him till one by one all the others find you."

"Ah! It is vairy amusing play!" cried Marie-Louise, slapping her hands. She explained it to Edouard, and then they all drew straws for who was going to be the one to hide. (Real straws—another advantage of being on a farm.) It was Gerard who drew the short straw, so he was "it." Had Jodie fixed it, holding the straws in a certain secret way? Almost certainly.

"OK!" said Jodie. "Gerard, you go off somewhere and hide."

Gerard shrugged and looked useless, though delicious.

"Bof! Where?" he asked, looking round.

"Anywhere!" said Jodie. "Any of these fields, in the barns, the woods—anywhere you like. My uncle's got a hundred and fifty acres," she said, sounding posh and rich. "We'll wait for ten minutes. Then we'll be coming to find you! We'll all go into the girls' tent so we can't see where you're going."

Jodie ushered them all into the tent, rather like a sheep-dog, and zipped the flap firmly shut.

"Fred!" she said. "You time us. Ten minutes, OK?"

"Why me?" protested Fred. "I'm already exhausted." He flopped down on Jess's sleeping bag and closed his eyes. Everybody else sat down. Edouard sneezed, then blew his nose. Marie-Louise cleaned her fingernails and chatted about "ze beautifool English countryside." Flora rubbed some anti-insect cream on her flawless arms. Jess passed the time by choosing a new ringtone—one that sounded like a microscopic Latin American samba band trapped inside a washing machine.

"Right!" said Fred. "Time's up!" Jess tucked her phone away safely under her pillow, and they all piled out of the tent. For a moment they hesitated. There were so many directions they could take: fields and woods and barns galore—if you like that sort of thing. And right now, Jess couldn't think of anything more convenient. Within minutes, probably, she would be cuddling up with Gerard under some divine and very private bush.

"Scatter, scatter!" cried Jodie, running off up the field towards the house and barns. She sounded like an army captain in the SAS. "We've got to separate!"

Jess plunged down towards the stream. She was sure Gerard would be down in that direction somewhere. After all, that was where they had flirted with their fingers in the mud. The place was already sacred to her. She would have a plaque put up: nailed to a tree. *HERE JESS JORDAN FELL UNDER GERARD'S SEXY SPELL.*

Jess arrived at the sacred spot, grabbed the hanging rope, and swung across the stream. The other side was quite steep and rocky and led up to an inviting little wood.

Jess was sure Gerard was waiting up there, with open arms. She toiled up the steep bank, breaking into an unattractive sweat. Never mind. Gerard would be sweaty, too. She wouldn't mind. In fact, she would bottle his sweat and sell it to younger girls. Jess reached the top of the bank, paused, sniffed her armpits suspiciously, and then entered the wood. Thick undergrowth and brambles pulled at her clothes and hair. At first it all seemed part of an enchanted game.

"Leave me alone, you horny thorny beasts!" she giggled. "We're just not meant for each other. You're a vegetable, and let's face it, I'm an animal. It would never work. And anyway, I wouldn't want to have buds till I'd had a career."

But after about ten minutes it started to get tiresome. By now Jess was out of breath, hot and bothered. She paused, and listened. Birds were singing in the canopy above. But there was no sign of Gerard. Maybe, if Gerard had come this way, he'd have left evidence. A fabulous French footprint in the mud or a path of lucky old crushed undergrowth leading to his hiding place. But there was nothing.

Jess paused. She was beginning to feel massively pissed off. She was definitely not going to find Gerard here. In fact, it would be a miracle if she found her way back. Dammit, dammit!

Gerard, you idiot, she thought. *Why didn't you hide up here? We could be halfway through our twentieth kiss by now.* Jess turned and floundered among the trees for about twenty minutes.

Suddenly, up ahead, she saw a bush move. She froze. Had she imagined it? She watched. It definitely twitched. Something alive was in that bush. Jess braced herself. Maybe it was Gerard. But maybe it was a fox, badger, deer—whatever wild things hung out here. Jess prepared to be bitten. Preferably by Gerard.

"Hello?" she called softly. "I can see you!" The bush shook slightly.

"'Allo?" came a reply. It sounded French. Jess's heart leapt in excitement.

"Gerard?" she called again. "Is it you?" The bush shook violently. Somebody backed out in a chaos of crackling branches and twigs. Disaster! It was Edouard.

25

"Edouard!" cried Jess, trying to hide her total horror and dismay. "What are you doing, hiding? You're supposed to be looking for Gerard." Edouard frowned at her and shrugged with total blank incomprehension.

"It's OK, it's OK," said Jess quickly. It wasn't his fault he hadn't understood the game. It wasn't his fault she had headed straight for his hiding place. It wasn't his fault he had failed to understand what she'd just said. None of it was his fault. She just might have to murder him all the same, though. Life was tough sometimes.

"I ham perdu," said Edouard. Jess raised her finger to her lips.

"Shhh!" she said, and managed to crank up a totally synthetic smile. God knows what "I ham perdu" meant. Why did he have to make conversation at a time like this? Didn't he realize they were in a deep crisis? They were lost in the goddamn wood, for God's sake. This was no time for all that "I ham perdu" business.

Jess beckoned in pantomime style. There was no point in trying to find Gerard now. He couldn't possibly have come up this way. They were already miles and miles away from the campfire. Possibly in another county. Possibly in another country. Wales, for instance. And even if they found Gerard, Jess's chances of a French-kissing lesson were nil, now that Edouard was hanging about talking about ham.

There was only one sensible course of action. They had to get back to the campfire and those lovely cozy tents before night fell and the werewolves came out. Jess led the way back, in vaguely what she imagined must be the right direction. After a while the ground started to slope a bit again. This, surely, must lead back down to the stream. Jess hated nature now. She just wanted all this vegetation removed and replaced with nice level pavements, pizza parlors, and, best of all, a bus route.

It ought to be better having Edouard with her for company, but somehow it made it worse. It was just awful being marooned with him in a wilderness. If they'd been at home, at least he could have done the decent thing and locked himself in his room while she watched TV downstairs.

Eventually they found themselves at the edge of the wood, and, looking down, Jess could see the stream glinting below. It must be the same stream, but it wasn't the same place where she and Gerard had held hands. It was a different field, further along the valley, or something. God! How she hated geography!

"The stream," she said, and immediately regretted it. Edouard unleashed a stream of his own: a tumbling, splashy flood of French words. It sounded a bit like, "Honor truvila rivvy air may honor purrpar traversila." He'd flipped. It wasn't French now. It was a Hobbity version of Elvish.

"I couldn't agree more," said Jess. She particularly liked the sound of "purrpar" and was already planning to have a kitten called just that. But first they had to get back to civilization before dying of exposure. Just to get out of the wood and down to the stream, they were going to have to push their way through a dense hedge of thorns and clamber over some strands of rusty barbed wire.

Jess took a deep breath, and began to move slowly forward through the brambles. Eventually, badly scratched and by now in a vile mood, she arrived at the barbed wire. Suddenly Edouard sprang forward, taking the initiative.

"Jerper ton ear sa poor tassistay," he said.

"I can't argue with that," said Jess. Masterfully Edouard grabbed the top strand of wire and held it up, and placed his cute little right foot on the lower strand and trod it down. This created a kind of aperture through which Jess was able to crawl. *My God!* thought Jess. *He does have his uses after all.*

Perhaps it was just as well she hadn't murdered him

awhile back. She held the wire for him to crawl through, but somehow, as she was letting go afterwards, the wire kind of sprang back cruelly at her and anchored in her sleeve.

"Ow!" yelled Jess.

"*Merde!*" said Edouard. Carefully he disentangled her. She pulled up her sleeve and examined her arm. The rusty barbed wire had given her a nasty little scratch. It was bleeding.

Suddenly, and startlingly, Edouard grabbed her arm, bent down, and sucked the wound, then spat it out. Jess was stunned. Was he a vampire or something? Then he let go of her arm and from the left pocket of his jeans he produced a handkerchief that, weirdly, was spotlessly clean. He shook it out and tied it round her arm, without ever looking her in the eye or saying a word.

"Honor purrpar lessay sallair," he said, with a certain grim microscopic expertise. Jess didn't understand a word. But it was obvious he had, in some Hobbity kind of way, saved her from a slow death by blood poisoning or something. She felt obscurely touched. Just as long as he didn't try to take things further and demand a whole afternoon playing doctors and nurses when her mum was out.

They climbed down the steep bank towards the stream. It looked deeper and more dangerous than the bit of stream at the bottom of the camping field. Jess was boiling with rage. How had they got into this mess? They weren't little kids, for God's sake. Why hadn't they just stayed around the campfire, doing charades and being mellow?

Whose stupid idea had all this been? Jodie's, of course. She obviously had wanted a chance to get Gerard on his own. The cunning bitch! (*Sorry, God,* she thought, *but sometimes you just have to let rip.*)

They stood and glared at the stream. There was no rope here. There weren't even stepping-stones. They were going to have to wade to the other side. It wasn't their camping field across there, it was a different field, but Jess guessed that the campsite couldn't be very far away because she could smell woodsmoke. Unless it was somebody else camping—the annual field trip of the Mass Murderers' Association, possibly? It would be just her luck.

She sat down and took off her shoes, swearing quite horribly out loud. It didn't seem to matter—Edouard wouldn't understand anyway. He also sat down and took off his shoes and socks. Jess ripped off her socks, got up, and picked her way gingerly to the water's edge. She didn't even look at Edouard. She didn't want to discuss it. Not in Elvish, anyway.

She dipped a toe in. Ow! It was freezing! Her foot almost fell off in shock. Still, there was nothing for it: no other way to get back. Jess set off, stepped on a sharp stone, lost her balance, lurched, and fell, with a strange terrible squeak, into the water.

Oh my God! she thought. *I'm going to drown. I didn't even manage to scream properly. And worst of all, Edouard is watching and I can't be looking my best.* Of all deaths, drowning was the one she dreaded most. She had hoped to die in about ninety years' time, in private, in a four-poster bed in Hollywood, attended by a posse of adoring young men in white silk livery.

And now this. She would arrive in the afterlife, spluttering her guts out, garlanded with frogspawn and crowned with a veil of green slime.

26

Jodie est un COW.

She felt a hand grab her. The hand was tiny but strong. Edouard had rescued her—again. As she struggled to her feet, Jess realized that the water was only about knee-high after all. But as she fell, she'd dropped her shoes and socks, and one sock, still rolled in a sort of ball, sailed off merrily downstream as if it was having a whale of a time, and disappeared around the corner.

Jess retrieved the other sock and her shoes, dragged herself to the bank, and hauled herself out, hanging on to Edouard and dripping and shivering. In addition to her previous injuries, she was now wet through, and her feet were cut by stones and covered in mud. She had been comprehensively beaten up by nature. She would never leave the town again.

She sat down on the bank, too massively furious even to swear. Edouard offered her his socks. She looked up. He wasn't smiling. He was just being seriously practical.

"Take," he said sternly. Jess hardly dared to disobey. Since they had been lost, Edouard had gradually acquired a certain authority. "Take," he said again, forcing his socks on her. Jess smiled wanly and put them on. He was trying to look after her, bless his little cotton socks. Quite literally.

Edouard put on his trainers, and Jess tied her shoelaces. *Oh well*, she thought. *I suppose nothing worse can happen now.* Then they got up and turned round, ready for the long haul up the field. And that was when they saw the cattle. A *whole herd of cattle* had appeared and was staring down at them.

They were only about fifty meters away. Perhaps there was a bull! Perhaps they were all bulls! Jess's heart soared up her throat like a skyrocket and actually appeared briefly in her mouth, pulsating away like a parasitic alien in a science fiction movie. She swallowed it. It tasted worse than anything.

She knew it was important not to look scared, but on the other hand, she was right on the very verge of pooing her pants. There was a hedge about a hundred meters away. She could smell the smoke of a campfire somewhere beyond it. She didn't really care if it was the Mass Murderers' Annual outing, now. Anything was better than being gored by a pack of mad cows.

Jess set off in a crazy, lurching run towards the hedge. She hadn't meant for it to be lurching, but the ground was strewn with rocks, big coarse tufts of grass, and fresh cow-pats gleaming in the evening light. Jess could hear the cattle following at a frisky trot.

She was vaguely aware that Edouard had got left behind. Maybe he was being gored right now! She ought to stop and look round, just to see if he was OK. Jess tried to look back over her shoulder while still running forward—never a good idea. She saw Edouard some distance behind her. He was surrounded by cattle but still on his feet. She tripped on a rock and landed in a gigantic cowpat.

It could have been worse. It could have been a facedown situation. The cow poo was "only" all down one side of her top and jeans. Jess scrambled to her feet again and raced as fast as she could to the hedge. But it was impossible to get through. The hedge had been reinforced with barbed wire.

French Exchange Partners Gored on Camping Trip, she thought. *"We're Having a Bilingual Joint Funeral," Says French Teacher*. Maybe a drowning wouldn't have been so bad after all.

Jess turned, panting, to face her doom. The cattle were a short distance downhill from her, but still following. Edouard was facing them. Suddenly he gave a weird high-pitched shriek and ran at them, waving his arms and shrieking a wide variety of French words at them, like a banshee.

The cattle didn't seem to like it. They came to a halt, turned tail, and thundered off down the meadow. Jess breathed a deep sigh. A wave of relief crept over her. Edouard had now rescued her three times. It was almost biblical.

OK, she was battered, bruised, gouged by barbed wire, and scratched by thornbushes. She was wet, had lost a sock, her clothes were saturated, and she was covered with cow dung. But let's face it, nothing is worse than being chased by a pack of large animals. Jess decided she was going to give up that fantasy about the football team.

Edouard joined her. He only seemed a bit out of breath. Jess gave him what she hoped was a grateful smile.

"Thanks," she said. "To be honest, I have a little bit of a thing about being gored by herds of mad cattle. Silly of me, I know, but the girl can't help it." She shrugged in what she hoped was a friendly matter.

"Jaypassay dayvaconss alla compagngngne," said Edouard. Luckily this statement did not seem to require an answer. Jess just nodded and, in an attempt to convey her gratitude, gave him the thumbs-up. He gave the thumbs-up in return and they exchanged a genuine smile for the first time in their relationship.

I wouldn't go so far as to call it lurve, thought Jess, with a secret giggle, *but we seem to have got over the murderous hatred stage.*

They walked uphill along the side of the hedge. Surely sooner or later they would come to a gate? How had the cattle got in there? Dropped by helicopter? Not unless farming methods had changed a lot since her childhood storybook *Old MacDonald*.

Eventually they did indeed come to a gate, and climbed over it without sustaining any injury. Perhaps their luck was changing? Yes! There, thank God, was the campfire. She could see hunched figures round its cheerful blaze.

The others noticed Jess and Edouard and made kind of

silly whooping noises to indicate that they had possibly been indulging in secret, sexy hanky-panky.

Jess ignored them and just limped towards the fire. Gerard was going to see her covered in cow poo and flayed alive with thorns, but frankly she was past caring.

"I love your new look!" cried Fred in a high-pitched camp voice, as she drew near. "My dear! It must have cost a fortune! But it suits you!"

"Oh my God!" cried Marie-Louise. "Poor Jess! You are dirty!" She got up and started flapping about in a pointless but sympathetic manner. Jodie, for some reason, looked absolutely furious.

"Have you seen Gerard or Flora?" she demanded. *Gerard and Flora?* A terrible idea flashed across Jess's mind.

"Aren't they back yet?" she asked, peering around in the semi-dark. She could only see Jodie, Marie-Louise, and Fred.

"Well, I can't see them here, can you?" snapped Jodie. "Nobody could find Gerard, so eventually we all came back here, except Flora. Presumably she found him. If they don't come back soon it'll be dark. Your phone rang twice—maybe she's sent you a text."

Jess hurried to the tent, grabbed her phone, and collected the messages. The first was from her mum, asking if she was warm enough. The second was indeed from Flora.

HI BABE, it said. **FOUND GERARD BUT WE GOT LOST. OK NOW. HUING T WITH NICE OLD BID. SEZ SHE'LL LEND US A TORCH. DON'T WAIT UP! LU FLO XXX**

Jess went back to the campfire and conveyed Flora's message. Jodie almost exploded.

"Got lost?" she snapped. "They got *lost*?!? They weren't supposed to go off together! That's just typical of Flora! She's a total airhead!"

There was a brief, embarrassed silence. Everybody was thinking the same thing, but nobody dared speak. Even Fred kept his mouth shut.

"Poor Jess is in bad state," said Marie-Louise. "Maybe she can takes a bath in you aunt's 'ouse, Jodie?"

"Sure, whatever," said Jodie, shrugging. "C'mon then."

Jess followed Jodie up the field towards the house. The lights were on, and the windows shone in the blue evening air. They were the color of orange juice: cheerful, inviting. But in Jess's heart there was no light, only a deep, impenetrable blackness. Could the day have turned out any worse? She doubted it.

✳ 27 ✳

Mon HEART est BROKEN!

s she showered, Jess's mind whirled with possibilities. Why would Flora and Gerard have gone off together? There could be only one reason. And the slightly festive air of Flora's text message confirmed it: **DON'T WAIT UP!** Jess tried to imagine what it would be like to wander down darkening lanes with Gerard, possibly hand in hand . . . Bliss! But *she* was the one he'd flirted with earlier, down by the stream. He'd actually *held her hand*, for God's sake. Did that count for nothing?

Washed, dried, and dressed in fresh clothes, Jess emerged. Jodie's uncle had come in and his wife was bustling about, making his supper. Betsy looked up from her basket and waved her tail in a bored and idle way. That dog was a total couch potato. For a split second Jess wished she could join Betsy in her basket. It seemed cozy and safe in the farm kitchen. But she knew she had to go out into the howling wilderness and confront her worst nightmares.

"I'll hang your washing in the utility room when it's ready, Jess," said Mrs. B. "Oh—you should take one of those torches by the door, and watch your step."

Jess thanked her, picked up a torch, and stepped out into the night. On her way down to the field, she met another light bobbing up towards her. It was Fred.

"I'm on my way to the loo," he said. "The Babes in the Wood have returned. It's all a big mystery. Jodie's grown long yellow fangs. We're marooned in some gothic fairy tale. I might have to chop your feet off by dawn."

"Fine, go for it," replied Jess. "I've never liked them. I'd rather have a set of wheels, to be honest."

"Oh, and that other mystery," said Fred. "Our divorce. Delightful though it is, it did rather come out of the blue. Was that so you could become an item with your matchbox boy toy?"

No way was Jess going to reveal that she had hoped to get off with Gerard. It now seemed totally ludicrous.

"I just got sick of being married to you," said Jess. "The way you load the dishwasher is *so* irritating. And that sucking noise you make on your pipe—nauseating. Plus your slippers smell."

"Fair enough," said Fred. "It's the monastery for me, then. Fabulous! Can't wait."

"As for Edouard," added Jess, "we still find each other

disgusting. He did save my life three times on the hike home, but even when he sank his teeth into my arm you could tell he wasn't enjoying it."

"Who would?" said Fred. "Personally I would prefer to eat a live elephant. Starting at the back."

They punched each other briefly and then separated. Jess felt slightly better as she made her way down towards the campfire. But only for a few seconds. Then the nervousness kicked in. She was going to have to see Gerard, and try not to catch his eye. It would obviously be best just to ignore him: pretend that wonderful holding-hands-underwater moment had never happened.

Gerard and Flora were sitting side by side, but not too close together. They weren't actually touching.

"Oh, hi, Jess!" cried Flora as Jess arrived. She sounded slightly hysterical. Her voice came out a bit shrieky. "I heard you got lost and fell in a cowpat! So did we! Well, we got lost, but we were spared the cowpat, thank God. Are you OK?"

"Yeah, fine. It was quite bracing actually," said Jess, and sat down.

"Would you like a Coke, Jess?" asked Marie-Louise. She seemed to be playing hostess—probably because Jodie was scowling, sunk down deeply into her fleece with her mouth covered, glaring into the flames.

"Gerard hid in a wood, up past the house," said Flora. "I found him almost right away. And we waited and waited, but nobody came. And then we thought we could hear a waterfall. So we looked for it and got lost. In the end we came out on a strange road, and there was a cottage, and this little old lady gave us a cup of tea and told us how to get back."

"Old ladies are losing their touch," said Jess, forcing a joke. "She should have fattened Gerard up in a cage and kept you as a domestic slave." Jess was really gutted at the thought of Flora and Gerard sharing this romantic fairy-tale adventure so soon after he had held Jess's hand and gazed rapturously at her down by the stream. Jodie wasn't the only one whose heart was slightly broken.

Flora laughed, and her laugh was a bit nervous. A sudden, deep silence fell. It was clear Jodie was not going to speak again this evening—possibly ever again in her life.

Marie-Louise was putting another log on the fire. Jess refused to focus on the charismatic blur that was Gerard. Edouard was playing with his Game Boy. Eventually Fred returned, a bobbing light in the dark.

"Are you Fred Parsons or a ghost?" said Jess. Well, somebody had to talk.

"I am the ghost of Fred Parsons," said Fred, and sat down by the fire.

"God! I hope this place isn't haunted," said Flora, with a nervous laugh. "Is your auntie's house haunted, Jodie?" As an attempt to force Jodie to speak, it had a certain charm. But Jodie just shrugged.

"Oh! I 'ope not!" laughed Marie-Louise. "I hate zat sort of thing."

"My granny is convinced she can communicate with the spirit of my grandpa," said Jess. "She even heard him speak out loud to her the other day."

"Oh, how weird!" said Flora. "Can we talk about this to-morrow? It's kind of spooky in the dark."

"I had a gerbil once who died," said Fred. "I wonder if I could contact his spirit and apologize for the dreary life he led in our house? They probably have pet mediums in California."

"Maybe the mediums themselves are animals," said Jess. "Maybe that sheepdog Betsy is a channel to the other side, receiving messages from the previous sheepdog."

"I'm sorry, Jess," said Marie-Louise, looking puzzled. "I don't h'understand what you are talking about."

"It's quite all right, old bean," said Jess. "Neither do I."

She wasn't doing very well at the witty repartee this evening. All she could think about was Gerard. It was a full-time job, avoiding looking at him. Her eyes were desperate just to have a little tiny peep. Oh no! They escaped from her control and whizzed over to where he was.

He was looking right at her. Her heart leapt. He smiled. Her bra melted. He gave a cute little shrug, almost as if to suggest that life was beyond one's control. Quickly Jess looked away. She didn't like that shrug. Life ought to be at least a teensy bit more under control than *this*.

"I think it's inspiring," said Flora. "Imagine being so in love with someone that you can still communicate with them after they've died." There was a brief, hanging silence. Marie-Louise sniffed. Communication among the living seemed more or less to have dried up.

"Well," said Jodie suddenly, "I'm going to bed. Fred, you're in charge of the fire." Fred looked startled. "Douse it down or something when everybody goes to bed." She stomped off to the tent and, if it had been possible to slam a tent door, she would have slammed it. She had to make do with the faint thwack of canvas and a nasty waspish swish of the zip.

"Well, it would appear to be time for silly songs," said Fred. "But I've mysteriously lost the will to live."

"Let's have one more Coke," said Flora. "Oh, they're warm! Horrid! I'll take a couple of bottles down to the stream." She got up. Gerard leapt up also.

"I will go wiz you," he said, chivalrously taking the bottles from her. No doubt their fingers brushed excitingly for a moment. Flora picked up a torch.

"Won't be long," she said awkwardly, and they strolled off down the hill.

"Right! That's it!" said Fred, getting to his feet. "Bedtime. Without violent movies on TV there is no reason to stay up late." He went off to the boys' tent.

Edouard scrambled to his feet and followed him, muttering something as he went. "Goo'night," possibly.

"I am going to bed, too, Jess," said Marie-Louise, looking a bit anxious. "But Fred has gone! What about ze fire?" She was such a mother figure.

"Flora can sort that out," said Jess acidly. "She's hot stuff." Jess felt quite scorched inside from Flora's latest bit of playing with fire.

In the girls' tent it was dark. Jodie was lying with her back to everybody, almost completely hidden in her sleeping bag. Jess and Marie-Louise got undressed in silence and slipped into their bags.

Jess lay for some time with her eyes open. The faint breathing noises and the creak of canvas, the sound of the wind in the trees and the occasional hoot of an owl outside were all, in theory, wonderful. But Jess was too upset to enjoy any of it. She just wished she was a million miles away. In fact, she wished she was at home. OK, she'd been bitten by a French boy, but hardly in the manner of her dreams or by the individual of her choice.

Eventually, Jodie started to snore. And Marie-Louise seemed to be asleep, too. Jess looked at her phone to check the time. An hour and a half had passed since Flora and Gerard went down the hill to cool their bottles of Coke. There hadn't been the sound of voices or any hint that they had returned. Jess hadn't had a wink of sleep. She could only lie there, her tummy tied in an agonizing knot, imagining Flora and Gerard down by the stream. They were probably—oh, kissing underwater by now. Beside her lay Flora's sleeping bag, empty and somehow taunting.

Suddenly somebody crept into the tent. It was Flora. Jess heard her undress and get into her bag. Flora snuggled in close and whispered, "Jess! Are you awake?"

Jess moved and whispered back, "Yeah. Can't sleep." Jodie was snoring and Marie-Louise was lying on her back with her mouth open. Privacy, of a sort, was available. Jess was lying with her back to Flora, but Flora leant over on her elbow and whispered right into her ear.

"Oh God, Jess, Gerard is amazing! I so, like, totally adore him! He says I've always been special. He says he noticed me right from the very first day they arrived in England. I can't wait to tell you all about it."

"Great," whispered Jess. She could certainly wait. It seemed her worst fears had come true, and her best plan for damage limitation was to try and pretend she was completely OK about it.

"I'll never be able to sleep," whispered Flora. "I'm tingling all over."

"Keep the sordid details to yourself," murmured Jess. "Us mere mortals have to get our shut-eye." But she knew that she was not going to get much sleep either.

"Back me up tomorrow if Jodie is pissed off with me," whispered Flora. It seemed that Jess not only had to accept that Gerard was now Flora's, but do a PR job on the situation as the best news since Romeo got with Juliet.

"OK," she croaked. She was going to have to dig deep tomorrow. She just hoped God would be watching. Gold stars for saintliness would have to be earned. Should she warn Flora that Gerard was a treacherous flirt and heartbreaker? Could she preserve a diplomatic silence? Or would she lose it, indulge in obscene shouting, and ruin everybody's weekend? The last seemed by far the most attractive option.

28

*J*ess woke early with cold feet. Birds were singing loudly all around the tent. Marie-Louise was getting dressed. Jess peeped out from her sleeping bag and noticed that, though when fully dressed Marie-Louise was a trifle homely, even nerdy, she seemed to be addicted to rather fabulous lacy underwear. Then Jess shut her eyes again, tight, and waited for Marie-Louise to finish dressing and leave the tent. Jess had no appetite for small talk, even about lingerie. She had noticed something else. Flora's sleeping bag was already empty.

This could only mean one thing. Presumably Flora hadn't slept much, tortured by thoughts of her Latin lover. She

must have tiptoed out just before daybreak, probably because she had a date with lover boy, wandering hand in hand under the trees and listening, enchanted, to the dawn chorus.

Eventually Marie-Louise left the tent and Jess struggled heavily out of her sleeping bag, like a hippo stuck in a swamp. *Well,* she thought, *I hope Flora's enjoyed her last twelve hours of bliss, because today She Must Die.* Jess was planning to kill Flora after breakfast—or possibly even during breakfast—with the nearest fatal implement. Has anybody ever been murdered with a nonstick spatula? Well, Flora could be the first. Strange how the arrival of a gorgeous boy could make you suddenly hate your best friend.

Jess dived into several jumpers and a fleece. These spring mornings were still kind of chilly—at least if you didn't have a hot date to keep you warm. Then she tiptoed out of the tent, leaving Jodie still lying rolled up in her sleeping bag. Jess didn't want to wake her. Somehow Jodie managed to convey the fact that, though asleep, she was still sulking and would continue to do so for the rest of the weekend.

Fred and Marie-Louise were fussing about around the fire. There was no sign of Gerard and Flora. Edouard was just coming out of the boys' tent, pulling on a hoodie. He grinned and gave her the thumbs-up sign.

"Good merning," he said.

"Hi, Ed!" said Jess. They seemed almost friends now. However, although she had been dumped by Gerard, Jess hoped Edouard wouldn't get any ideas. He had to be satisfied with a friendly grin. That was about as far as she wanted to take things. OK, he had already sucked on her arm. But it had been a medical procedure and in no way implied that they might become an item.

"Well, though I say so myself, I think I've whipped up a fabulous little fire!" cried Fred in a queeny swooping voice, flapping his hands about. "It's a *camp*fire, obviously, which is why it's that wonderfully chic pink and gold color, with sparkly bits all round the edges!"

"Would you like ze scrambled egg, Jess?" asked Marie-Louise. She was such a sweetheart. "Wiz bacon and tomates?"

"You bet!" said Jess. "Stick it in the pan. Go for it." Marie-Louise smiled happily. Though back home in France she only ever had a croissant in the mornings, she had taken to "Ze English Breakfast" with gusto. And, to be honest, gutso.

"Did you see Flora this morning?" Jess asked Fred.

"Strangely and bizarrely," said Fred, "I didn't. And Gerard's also missing. Perhaps they've been kidnapped by the fairies."

"One does hope so," said Jess. "And one can only hope they've turned Flora into a fat old pig with a snout covered in bristles. It's what she so richly deserves."

"Jess," said Marie-Louise, "pliz could you cut up ze tomates?"

Jess and Fred helped Marie-Louise cook an enormous breakfast. Edouard went off on a little walk to collect wood, mainly because he knew there would be sexy beetles hiding beneath every log. There was still no sign of Jodie.

"Should we wake Jodie?" asked Marie-Louise, as breakfast neared completion.

"I think she's died of disappointment," said Jess, gazing

lustfully at the creamy panful of scrambled eggs. Marie-Louise was a great cook. She looked a bit worried, though.

"Is Jodie . . . angry wiz Flora?" she whispered. "Because of Gerard?"

Jess nodded and tried to look as if the whole thing was vastly entertaining. Secretly, of course, her own heart was breaking, but she knew she'd feel a whole lot better once she had a plateful of breakfast inside her.

"Leave her," said Jess. "If the smell hasn't woken her up, she doesn't deserve any breakfast."

Marie-Louise hesitated. She was about to divide the food. She looked around. Then she frowned and pointed down towards the stream.

"Flora and Gerard!" she said. "Oh no! Zere is not enough breakfast . . ."

Flora and Gerard were indeed visible in the distance— Flora was swinging across the stream on the rope, and Gerard was waiting to catch her. Jess saw the exact moment when Flora kind of fell into his arms, and stayed there for what seemed like six years. Eventually they turned round and started walking up the hill, hand in hand.

"They don't deserve any stinking breakfast!" said Jess. "Come on, Marie-Louise. You, me, Fred, and Ed—if they want some, they can cook it themselves."

Marie-Louise still looked guilty and anxious. Jess grabbed the pan from her and ladled out the scrambled egg onto four plates. Then she divided the bacon and tomatoes. Edouard arrived and plonked a load of logs down nearby.

"Flora!" called Marie-Louise, as the wandering lovers

arrived. "Gerard! I'm sorry, I did not know . . . zere is not enough breakfast."

"Oh, don't worry about that!" answered Flora, smiling a secret smile and tossing her hair back like a blonde in a shampoo ad. She and Gerard were obviously too fabulously and romantically happy to need mere food. "We're not hungry, are we, Gerry?"

Gerard looked a bit surprised for a moment and then shook his head. You could tell he was just dying to eat a whole raw pig and a dozen eggs straight from a hen's bum.

"We've been on a lovely walk," said Flora, sitting down next to Jess as if they were still best friends. Gerard sat down next to Flora on the other side. This meant Jess did not have to look at him, which suited her just fine. Once they'd sat down, Flora and Gerard started holding hands again. For a moment Jess felt a wave of nausea, but heroically she conquered it and went back to her egg.

"Where's Jodie?" asked Flora, looking around.

"Still in the arms of Morpheus, as the saying goes," said Fred. "Who was Morpheus, by the way?"

"I don't know," said Jess. "But he certainly gets around. Everyone's always in his arms. Evidently a hideous flirt." She hoped Gerard would feel the sting of this sarcastic aside, but he was busy playing with Flora's fingers and clearly not listening.

"Morpheus is ze god of sleep!" said Marie-Louise. Though a sweetheart, she could also be something of an irritating swot.

"Mind if I scrounge a little tiny bit of your bacon, babe?" said Flora in an affectionate aren't-I-cute kind of way.

"Sure, help yourself," said Jess. This was a translation of *Can't you keep your thieving mitts off anything, you tart?* But of course Flora didn't know that.

Flora broke Jess's piece of bacon in half (half! Yes, a whole *half!*). Then she dipped it in ketchup; then she used it to scoop up a big dollop of scrambled egg—the very bit Jess was particularly looking forward to eating.

"Mmmmm!" said Flora.

"Have some more," said Jess. "Go on! Get stuck in! Don't mind me!" She nearly managed to make it sound like a friendly joke rather than a savage howl. But Flora didn't notice either way. She was hardly listening, either. Nothing Jess ever said could possibly be of interest to her from now on.

Flora had taken the first bite herself: now she fed the second bit to Gerard. He opened his mouth, giving Flora an adoring sideways look. She popped the lot in his mouth, and even removed a smear of ketchup from his chin and sucked it off her finger. Gross! Jess's own mouthful of bacon and egg started to taste like dirty socks and damp cardboard.

"We saw some lovely birds this morning," said Flora. As if they were just a couple of mad birdwatchers and they'd only sneaked off before dawn to ogle thrushes and stuff. Whereas really they'd been sticking their tongues down each other's throats in a way birds would find totally disgusting.

I just hope they give each other glandular fever, thought Jess.

"Oh, I love ze birds also!" trilled Marie-Louise.

"Personally I prefer the giant cane toads of Australia,"

said Fred. "Apparently they explode with the most delightful bang if you run over one."

"Ugh, Fred, shut up!" hissed Jess. "Some of us mere mortals are trying to eat what's left of our breakfast!" Jess concentrated hard on her breakfast and gobbled the rest of it up before Flora and Gerard could steal any more.

Just as she finished, Flora stood up and said she was going to nip to the loo. Jess got up, too.

"I'll come with you," she said. She urgently had to say something to Flora and when else was she going to get the chance? The girls' tent was no good. Jodie was still in there. And Jess could see that for the rest of the day, Flora would be fastened to Gerard's side.

They walked up the hill and past some low bushes that screened the campsite from the farmhouse. Flora had grabbed Jess's arm and was clinging on tight. She glanced over her shoulder to make sure they couldn't be overheard.

"Oh, God, Jess, Gerard is so amazing!" she whispered. "He's just, like, totally wonderful. And I know this is crap, but he says I'm the most beautiful girl he's ever seen!"

Jess pulled her arm fiercely out of Flora's grasp, stood stock-still, and glared at her.

"Do you realize that you're totally ruining this entire weekend for everybody?" she demanded. "Jodie's, like, so furious she won't even come out of her tent, and it's really embarrassing for everybody the way you two keep going off together. For God's sake have a bit of tact and stop all that goddamn groping and licking each others' fingers and stuff—at least in public. At least until the end of this camping trip."

Flora frowned. She blushed. Her eyes, normally a gentle, transparent blue, flashed like a storm over the Mediterranean.

"What's got into you?" she demanded. "I thought you'd be pleased for me. Jodie doesn't own Gerard. I'll go out with anyone I like, and if you can't cope with that, tough!"

And she stomped off to the outdoor loo, went in, and slammed the door. Jess was still full of fury. She could almost feel steam pouring out of her ears. What now? Should she march up to the loo and continue the row through the locked door? Should she tell Flora that less than twenty-four hours ago Gerard had been holding *her* hand?

Would it be too cruel to break Flora's heart? thought Jess, her mind whirling. *Well, why not? After all, even if she doesn't know it, Flora's broken mine.*

* 29 *

GREEDY COW!!

FAT FRENCH ARSE!!

eething with rage, Jess marched back down to the campfire. Marie-Louise was talking fast in French to Gerard in an intense, private kind of way. It sounded a bit like a pep talk or something. Edouard looked embarrassed and was fiddling with a beetle in a matchbox. Fred caught Jess's eye, and pulled a face which she instantly understood. It meant: *What's going on? Do I sense tension? Is something dangerous about to happen? Why are the hairs standing up on the back of my neck?*

Jess raised her eyebrows as if to say, *Don't ask me. I would never make a fool of myself with a ludicrous French lover boy.* Marie-Louise stopped talking urgently to Gerard, as if she didn't want Jess to overhear. Although God knew, Jess's French was so poor she could more easily have understood the crazy cackling of a hyena. Jess sat down, trying to smile broadly at everybody, as if everything was totally fine.

"Right!" she said. "Great! So . . . what shall we do today? We've done hide-and-seek, we've done charades . . . ?"

"How about this great new fun thing called sleep?" said Fred. But as he said it, his face changed. He was looking over Jess's shoulder, and he suddenly went pale, as if King Kong had loomed up behind Jess. Quick as a flash, Jess whirled round. Jodie had just emerged from her tent. She was bundled up in a fleece and her hair was all over the place, just wild. Her eyes were flashing and her nostrils were flaring in high-voltage fury.

"Where the hell's my breakfast!?" she roared. The empty frying pan and the empty plates told their own story. Marie-Louise looked scared, and got up to her knees.

"I'll cook you some, Jodie," she said, and started scrabbling around in the "food store"—a little cluster of plastic boxes.

"So you ate it all, you greedy pigs?" growled Jodie, stomping towards the fire. The earth seemed to shake. Fred did a funny little pretend cringe to Jess, secretly. Gerard put on his shades and tried to look cool and uninterested. Edouard gawped, frightened to death.

"I was woken up by the smell of bacon frying, and guess what? There's none left!" Jodie stood by the fire and kicked a log. The fire sort of shifted and a few sparks flew up into the smoke.

"Oh no!" said Marie-Louise, ransacking the stores. "Zere

is no bacon left! But I can make you eggs and tomates, Jodie."

"Don't bother!" snapped Jodie. "It's only *my* field, after all. This whole trip was only *my* idea. The stinking bacon was only bought by *my* mum. Why should I have any breakfast?"

Marie-Louise looked puzzled. She was having trouble understanding Jodie's sarcasm. But Jodie's mood was clear. Marie-Louise's eyes filled with tears. Frenziedly she searched the plastic boxes, looking for some delicacy that would tempt Jodie out of her black mood and distract her from her obvious plan to eat everybody else alive.

Jess realized it was up to her to say something. The Frenchies couldn't defend themselves because they were, well . . . French. Fred would never get involved in any kind of row. Right now he had rolled over on his tummy and was pretending to read his Stephen King book.

"Chill out, Jodie," said Jess. "There's plenty of food. My mum packed some croissants. They're in that green tin."

"I don't want stinking croissants!" snapped Jodie, still standing over them. "They make me feel *sick!*" Sitting down, Jess felt at a disadvantage. It was like being bombed. She got up.

"There's no need to be so angsty about it!" said Jess. "It's only breakfast! If it's bacon you want, I'm sure we can get some more. Your auntie probably has some."

"I don't want to *disturb* my auntie!" said Jodie. "I don't want to be *cadging stuff* off her all the time. She's got a *medical condition!*" Jodie glared at Jess as if it was Jess's fault that the auntie was unwell.

"For God's sake, relax!" shouted Jess. She decided not to ask about Aunt Rose's medical condition, in case it was embarrassing or something. "Have some toast, some beans, whatever!" Marie-Louise was actually crying now. Gerard got up and strolled off down the field. "Jodie," Jess went on, more quietly, "you're upsetting everybody! Come on, get a grip! We're supposed to be the hosts and stuff! You've upset Marie-Louise!"

"*I'm upset!*" roared Jodie, so loudly you could hear the spit boiling in her throat. "What about *me*?"

At this point Flora returned from the loo, looking sour and rebellious. Jodie turned on her.

"Ah, the divine *Flora!*" she yelled. "I hear you ate all my stinking breakfast, you greedy *cow!*" Flora looked startled but indignant.

"I *so* didn't!" she snapped. "Ask Jess. I had literally, like, *no* breakfast at all. Gerard and I didn't feel like any. Tell her, Jess!"

"Well, I wouldn't say you had *no* breakfast, as such," said Jess. She was feeling angry with Flora as well as Jodie. "I seem to remember you nicking quite a lot of mine."

"I *so* didn't!" snarled Flora. "It was a tiny piece of bacon and a microscopic bit of egg about the size of a pea."

"It was half a rasher of bacon and a huge dollop of egg!" said Jess.

Suddenly Fred closed his book and jumped to his feet. He pretended to be holding a microphone and facing a TV camera.

"Hostilities broke out here in the early hours following a dispute over supplies," he said in a breathless reporter's voice. "The Red Cross have asked for a ceasefire at ten-thirty to bury the dead, evacuate the wounded, and so that everyone can go to the loo. This is Fred Parsons in the war zone at Walnut Farm, handing you back to the studio."

"Shut up, Fred. You're an *idiot*!" yelled Jodie.

"Fred's not an idiot!" shouted Jess. "You're the one who's behaving like an idiot!"

"Yes!" Flora added. "We're supposed to be looking after Marie-Louise and Ed and Gerry, not giving them a hard time!"

"Gerry?!" said Jodie, in a taunting voice. "Who the hell's *Gerry*?"

"Gerard," said Flora. "It's just a nickname. What's your problem?"

"For God's sake, chill out, both of you," said Jess. "This is supposed to be a fun weekend, not some kind of international incident!"

"I don't care!" shouted Jodie. "I hate France anyway!"

"Jodie! I have found some more bacon!" pleaded Marie-Louise, from a pile of ransacked plastic boxes. She held out a little parcel of bacon, wrapped in clingfilm. "Shall I cook it for you?"

"Go to hell!" shouted Jodie. "I don't want any stinking bacon! You can shove it up your fat French arse!" And she stomped off in the direction of her auntie's house.

There was a brief silence, during which Edouard scrambled to his feet and walked off towards the hedge and the infinitely preferable company of insects. You could tell he was trying not to run.

"Phew!" said Fred. "What's got into her?"

Jess could hardly believe that Fred didn't realize what had

got into Jodie. Had he just not noticed Flora and Gerard eating their breakfast off each other's bodies?

"PMS," said Jess, giving Flora an accusing look. Marie-Louise wiped her eyes. "Take no notice of Jodie," Jess said to Marie-Louise. "She always has these flare-ups."

"Flare-ups?" said Marie-Louise, in a trembly voice. "What is zat?"

Suddenly, abruptly, Flora walked off. Gerard was down by the river now, leaning against a tree and staring into the water. Maybe he was planning to do the decent thing and throw himself in. Flora was evidently rushing off to be with him, even through her own French exchange partner was in tears. Jess put her arm round Marie-Louise.

"It's fine, it's OK, don't cry," she said. But, somehow, Jess's kindness made Marie-Louise feel worse. She threw herself into Jess's arms and wept.

Jess looked over Marie-Louise's shoulder at Fred, who shrugged and backed off. He pulled another face, which meant: *I can't stand displays of girly emotion, so excuse me while I vanish for several hours.*

Jess glared at him. She so needed his support at this crucial moment: his jokes, his clumsy cleverness. But Fred just backed off and went on going, shrugging his shoulders and pulling faces. Jess gave him a furious glare—a promise that, at the first opportunity, she was going to give him hell. Once she'd finished giving hell to everybody else.

"Oh, Jess!" sobbed Marie-Louise. "I am zo un'appy!"

"Take no notice of Jodie," said Jess. "She's just a moody cow."

"It is not Jodie," said Marie-Louise. "It is somesing else!"

Jess braced herself. Whatever next?

✳30✳

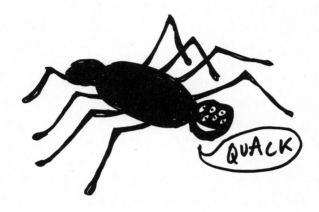

QUACK

"What's the matter, Marie-Louise?" said Jess. "Are you homesick or something?"

Marie-Louise shook her head and, between sobs, tried to come up with a sentence. Unfortunately her command of English seemed to be slipping.

"It is my—how you say . . . it is Miami," she said.

"Miami?" said Jess, puzzled. "What, like in Florida?" How could a French girl be upset by a random American city?

"No, no," sobbed Marie-Louise. *"Mon ami!"* Oh no! She was speaking French. This was totally unfair. So far, Marie-Louise had been the one French person with a great command of English.

"Wait!" said Jess. "I'll get my dictionary!"

"I go to toilet!" said Marie-Louise. "Excuse me one moment!"

She ran off towards the farm. Jess hesitated. Maybe Marie-Louise was ill. It certainly would be tiresome to be marooned on a camping trip if you weren't feeling great. Maybe there was an illness called Miami. Or Monami, or, whatever.

Whatever, she was still going to need that dictionary. Jess strolled over to the girls' tent. This trip was such hard work. Still, it must be ten times worse for Marie-Louise if she was feeling ill in a foreign country. Jess hoped she wouldn't catch Miami.

When Fred reappeared, they would have fun thinking of all the cities in the world that sounded like diseases. Seattle sounded a bit like a tummy upset. Kuala Lumpur. Rotterdam. Then they could spend some quality time thinking of diseases that sounded like cities. "I have a penfriend in Acne, Ohio." "We're holidaying in Candida this winter." That should help to pass the time. Ten minutes, anyway. This fabulous weekend, which they had fought so hard to create, was turning into an endless ordeal.

The idea of camping was supposed to involve a gang of mates having fabulous fun and laughter around the campfire. So where was everybody? Jodie had disappeared to the farmhouse. Gerard and Flora had disappeared somewhere down by the river. Marie-Louise had disappeared to the loo. Fred had just disappeared. Only Edouard was visible, creeping about by a distant hedge.

Jess heaved a great sigh and entered the girls' tent. Now,

where was the dictionary? She dropped down onto her knees on her sleeping bag, and suddenly saw it. Not the dictionary: a *spider*. A massive deadly black spider, *almost the size of her fist*. There it was, crouching evilly beside her pillow, grinning up at her, less than a meter away!

Jess almost fainted. She nearly had an attack of Rotterdam right there in the tent. A red-hot rocket of terror scorched up her throat. For an instant she was paralyzed with fear; then she kind of shot back through the tent door like a film being played backwards.

"Help!" she tried to scream, but who was going to help? Who was going to get rid of the spider before Jess actually died of fright? There was only one person available: Edouard.

"Ed!" called Jess, running towards him. As she ran, she realized that for once, fate had dealt her a couple of aces. The only person around was Edouard. But Ed was the very man for the job. Ed was, after all, seriously into creepy-crawlies. He looked up as she hurtled towards him.

"Ed!" she gasped, arriving. "There's a spider in my tent!" Ed frowned. Oh no! She'd forgotten that he didn't speak English!

"A spider!" she shouted.

"Quack?" said Edouard.

What? He's quacking at me, thought Jess. *No, it can't be, I must have dreamed it.*

"A spi-der!" she repeated.

"Quack?!" said Edouard.

He really is quacking, thought Jess. *He's turning into a goddamn duck. This has to be a dream.*

"Spider in tent!" said Jess in desperation.

"Quack?" said Edouard. Then he did the best thing ever. He produced his dictionary. Jess grabbed it. Hands shaking, she turned over the pages and found the entry: *spider: araignée*. She pointed out the word, then pointed to the tent.

"*Araignée* in tent!" she yelled. "Help, please! Get rid of *araignée*!"

Edouard's face lit up with huge delight. He ran off towards the tent as if there was a big boxful of chocolate biscuits waiting for him there. Jess followed warily. She was certainly not going to accompany Ed. He was on his own.

He disappeared into the tent. Jess stayed outside. There was a pause and little rustling sounds from within.

"Journer purrpar latroovee!" he called. Oh no. Not that again. He'd gone off into Elvish.

Jess peeped in gingerly through the door. Edouard was lifting up the sleeping bags and peering under them.

"Find, Eddie!" said Jess. She was just going to ignore whatever Ed said and simply say things of her own. "Fetch! Good dog!"

Suddenly Edouard became still. He was staring into the far corner, by Jodie's rucksack. Jess froze. Edouard dived. He caught it—actually in his fingers—*yeaurch!*—and transferred it into one of his little boxes. Then he came out, beaming with joy. He put the box in his pocket. Jess simply could not imagine how he could do such a thing. Forget France— this guy was from another planet.

"*C'est magnifique!*" he said. Even Jess knew what that meant.

"*Merci!*" she said, and patted him on the back. Not in an

amorous way at all. Just the kind of way you might pat a
jolly little dog. "Just one thing, though . . ." Jess somehow
couldn't help herself. "What was all that quacking business
earlier?"

"Quack?" said Edouard.

"You're doing it again!" said Jess. "Quack! What is
quack?"

"Quack?" said Edouard.

At this point, luckily, Marie-Louise arrived. She had
clearly spent a few minutes in the loo, doing deep breathing
and stuff, and was now more in control of herself.

"Marie-Louise," said Jess, "What does *quack* mean?
Edouard keeps quacking at me."

"Ah!" said Marie-Louise. "*Quoi* means 'what' in English.
Like 'What did you say?'"

"Ah! I see," said Jess. "At least I've learnt one goddamn
word of French, so this weekend hasn't been totally
wasted."

"Quoi?" quacked Marie-Louise. Jess had spoken too fast.

"Nothing," said Jess. "Now tell me, Marie-Louise: What is
your problem?"

"Eet ees stupide," said Marie-Louise. Jess put her arm
round her, in what she hoped was a reassuring manner.
Gestures are kind of important when verbal communication
is tricky.

"I'm sure eet ees not stupide," said Jess. Oh no! She was
trying so hard to empathize with Marie-Louise, she had
started speaking with a cod French accent!

"Eet ees *mon ami*," said Marie-Louise. "My boyfriend.
Pascal."

"What ees wrong wiz 'eem?" inquired La Jess.

"My friends in France send me texts. Zey say ee ees wiz uzzair gairlz." Marie-Louise's voice was trembling, and her French accent was getting stronger and stronger. Any minute now she might plunge into Elvish.

Pascal was seeing other girls? *Ze bastarde! All boys are peegs!* thought Jess. *Oh no. I'm even thinking in a French accent now.* She had to reassure Marie-Louise, though. She didn't want to have to deal with any more of that French crying.

"Why don't you telefon to eem?" asked Jess. "Ask eem if eet ees true."

"My phone ees not workingue henny more!" cried Marie-Louise in despair. "Eet have no charge!"

"Well, borrow mine!" cried Jess, producing it with a flourish. Marie-Louise actually smiled. Then she grabbed hold of Jess and kissed her bouncily on both cheeks.

"Sank you, Jess!" she said. "You are vairy kind!"

"Off you go!" said Jess, recovering her English accent. "Phone him. Talk for as long as you like."

Jess staggered back to the fireside and threw another log on. She lay down on one of the blankets. Marie-Louise walked off down the field to find some privacy. Edouard had gone off to play with his fabulous state-of-the-art new spider. There was a moment of peace and quiet.

Jess closed her eyes. She felt shattered. Nothing was quite so tiring as emotional trauma. Except possibly emotional trauma in a foreign language. The warmth of the fire soothed her. The spring sunshine warmed her. Jess drifted off into a light doze. She knew she was still by the campfire, but she was deeply relaxed.

Suddenly she heard a footstep nearby. Maybe Marie-Louise had come back and was eager for more counseling. Selfishly, perhaps, Jess decided to pretend to be asleep. She kept her eyes firmly closed and tried to look deeply, blissfully asleep. Then somebody sat down beside her. Heavily.

"Right!" said Jodie's voice, sounding very tight and seething with poison. "I've decided I'm going to go home."

Jess's eyes snapped open. It seemed there was a brand-new crisis for her to deal with. Frankly, life would have been a lot more restful in a riot.

✳ 31 ✳

INSERT CUNNING PLAN HERE:

*J*ess sat up and, to gain a little time, rubbed her eyes. How was she going to calm Jodie down and turn her from a wounded lion into a cute playful kitten by the time Flora came back to the campfire? For a moment she thought how restful it would be if Jodie *did* go home. But no, it would be really awkward—after all, they were camping in Jodie's aunt's field.

If she flounced off home now, Jodie would be sulking all month: right through the Easter holidays and beyond. And after all, Jess was really fond of Jodie. When she was in a good mood she was loads of fun. And it must be really embarrassing, having your French exchange partner getting all loved up with somebody else when everybody knew you fancied him yourself. Jess could identify with this—and how.

"OK," she said. "Let me get my head round this. First things first. Have you had any breakfast?"

"Well, as a matter of fact," said Jodie, "I did grab a piece of toast in my auntie's kitchen."

"Great!" said Jess. "What did you have on it? Marmalade?"

"Well, if you really must know," snapped Jodie, "bacon."

"So you had a bacon sandwich!" Jess was beginning to feel jealous. "Great! With ketchup?"

"Oh, shut up about food, Jess," said Jodie. "You're such a pig. There are other things in life, believe it or not."

"Listen," said Jess, ignoring Jodie's insult, "I'm your fairy godmother. All my spells are at your disposal. What shall I do? Your wish is my command." Jodie still looked grumpy, but you could see she was considering the idea.

"Make elephants fly," she said eventually. "Make them fly in formation over Flora's head and dump on her, one by one."

"Certainly, it shall be done," said Jess. "And might we suggest—personal disfigurement as well? After all, elephant poo can be washed off, but huge nostrils like craters could last a lifetime." The vaguest hint of a smile crossed Jodie's face.

"Disfigurement, yes . . . ," she mused. "Let's give her the arse of an ogre."

"May I suggest the arse of a flatulent green ogre?" said Jess. "Green's very *now*. It's the new black. And possibly mossy green teeth to match?" Jodie grinned, and the grin stayed. Hmmm. This seemed to be working.

"Not that I would give up on black," said Jess. "Certainly, in the form of blackheads, they offer a very attractive option."

"All over her face!" enthused Jodie. "And instead of hair, she should have bristles."

"Scales?" suggested Jess. "With lashings of slime? And every time she opens her mouth, instead of words, a fart comes out?"

Jodie laughed. Actually laughed out loud. Jess felt a flush of triumph. Could she build on this change of mood? Could she complete the comedy therapy and coax Jodie towards kittenhood?

"God! I almost feel sorry for her!" said Jodie. Then she clenched her teeth and sort of growled. "Not quite, though."

"Someone I really do feel sorry for," said Jess, moving swiftly on, "is Marie-Louise. Apparently her boyfriend back in France is seeing other girls and she keeps getting texts warning her."

"Oh my God!" Jodie dropped her head in her hands for a moment. "Was I very rude to her?"

"Quite rude, I would say," said Jess, keeping the tone light. "On a scale of one to ten, nine and a half, probably. Something about shoving the bacon up her fat French arse . . . ?" Jodie groaned. "Speaking of which," Jess went on, "if you keep your eyes open next time she's getting ready for bed, you might get a glimpse of a gold lamé thong."

"Oh no!" Jodie groaned. "Here she comes. I'm about to grovel. But don't expect me to apologize to Flora. She deserves to fry in hell."

Jess didn't comment. She watched Marie-Louise walking towards them across the grass, and tried to tell from her body language whether she had been reassured or not by the call to her boyfriend.

"How did it go?" she asked as Marie-Louise arrived.

"I am not sure . . . he said eet was just lies, but . . ." Marie-Louise shrugged. "Until I can see 'im face to face . . . ? Thanks for borrowing me your phone, Jess." She gave it back. "But on ze phone—it is hard to communicate, yes?"

"It's very hard to communicate even face to face," said Jess. "Jodie wants to apologize to you for her temper tantrum earlier."

"Yeah," said Jodie. "I was totally out of order. Sorry. You have a fabulous arse." Marie-Louise looked alarmed, but faintly pleased.

"Yes, it's a lot smaller than either Jodie's or mine," added Jess. Marie-Louise smiled.

"Don't worry, Jodie," she said, blushing. "I h'understand you are h'upset."

"No, I'm fine about it now," said Jodie, rolling over onto her back—*almost* like a kitten that wants to have its tummy rubbed. "Gerard's got a perfect right to go off with Flora if he wants to. I hope they'll be very happy."

"Ooh, good!" said Marie-Louise. "Escuse me, I am a little cold. I go to get my jumpair." She went off to the tent.

"OK," said Jodie, in a low growly voice. "So that's the apology out of the way."

"Brilliant! Well done!" said Jess. "Now, for God's sake, don't go home. It really is great here. And if you go, it'll spoil it for everybody else. And you said yourself just now that Gerard's got a perfect right to go off with Flora if he wants to."

Despite mouthing these civilized words, Jess was secretly clenching her teeth in private rage. She wondered if Gerard had also treated Jodie to the wow factor. Had he held her hand and stared into her eyes and showered her with compliments before moving swiftly on?

"I only said that to make Marie-Louise feel better," muttered Jodie. "The only reason I'll stay—if I do stay—is if we can play some really ingenious trick on them."

She looked Jess straight in the eye. Basically this was an ultimatum. Jess had to go along with the idea. Possibly even supply the brilliant plan. "We've got to humiliate them both," Jodie went on, like a lion chewing a bone. "OK?"

Jess felt a knot of tension and stress gathering just behind her tummy button. OK, Flora had behaved badly—greedily grabbing Gerard without considering anybody or anything else. But after all, she was still Jess's best friend.

Should she warn Flora that Gerard had actually held hands with Jess only an hour or so before going off with Flora? If her new beau was a heartbreaker, didn't Flora have the right to know? And didn't she also have the right to know that Jodie was plotting a humiliating revenge? Jess sighed.

If she'd been the one to pull Gerard, Jess could imagine how easily the rest of the weekend, and the rest of the gang, might have become kind of irrelevant. In fact, the presence of other people would have been torment. Flora and Fred were Jess's two best friends on earth, but with Gerard's arm around her, and the prospect of several hours' snogging under some picturesque and solitary tree, well—friendship just might have had to take a backseat for a while.

This was so obviously what Flora was feeling, which was

why she and Gerard were so often absent at the moment. Where were they now? Wrapped around each other in an area of Outstanding Natural Beauty, probably. Jess's stomach sank with bitter jealousy.

"Think of a cunning plan," said Jodie. "You're the one with the brain cells. I want Flora and Gerard on toast by tonight. If I have to sit through another evening with them groping each other I won't be responsible for my actions." She stomped off towards the girls' tent, grabbed her towel, and headed for the farmhouse.

"I'm taking a shower," she called to Jess. "Get that thinking cap on! Remember, you're in training to be a wicked stepmother!"

I was supposed to be a fairy godmother, thought Jess. Marie-Louise emerged from the girls' tent, wrapped in a fleece. She sat down by Jess.

"It is wonderfool now zat Jodie is feelingue bettair," she said. "Isn't it?"

Poor deluded French person, thought Jess. *If only you knew*. But she made some encouraging noises and prodded the fire with a stick.

"Ah! Fred is coming now!" said Marie-Louise. Jess looked up. Fred was indeed climbing over a gate—the same gate that Jess had climbed last night, when she was wet and covered with cow poo. Fred was carrying his Stephen King book. "I love Fred!" said Marie-Louise. "He is h'amusing!"

Suddenly Jess realized that there was only one person here who could rescue her from this potentially explosive situation. It was Professor Fred.

*J*ess got up and ran across to Fred. He looked
alarmed. "What is it?" he said. "Has someone
died?"

"No, but unless we act fast, somebody's gonna."

"What?" Fred raised a quizzical eyebrow. "Why ever did I
leave my secret lair just now? I blame Stephen King. The bit
I was reading was making me feel sick and I felt I needed a
break."

"Listen!" said Jess. "Jodie's ordered me to think of a
cunning plan, and if I don't come up with something before noon she's going to bite my head off and spit it in
the stream."

"Compared to what's just happened in my book, a mild case of decapitation is really nothing to worry about," said Fred.

"Shut up, Fred! This is serious! Jodie wants to get revenge on Flora and Gerard, but I can't cook up a plan that's going to upset Flora, much as I hate her right now."

"Why do you hate her right now?" asked Fred. "The world of female emotion is so fast-moving."

Whoops! Jess's galloping mind screeched to a halt. Fred mustn't know that she'd ever fancied Gerard herself, let alone held hands with him. That really would be humiliation.

"Well, you know," she gabbled, "going off with this French loser instead of having fabulous laughs with me all weekend. He is *such* a moron."

"You've lost me," said Fred. "What's the issue? In words of one syllable or preferably one letter."

"Jodie's in a hissy fit about Flora and Gerard," said Jess. "Mostly because she fancies him herself. So she's ordered me to think up a horrid trick to play on them. But I can't do that, because Flora and I are supposed to be best mates. So I'm asking you to lay on something that will distract Jodie."

"To, er, lay on something?" faltered Fred. "Karaoke? A flight in an air balloon? A champagne supper at the Ritz?"

"Exactly," said Jess. "Preferably all three. Get it organized, Parsons, or I'll think of a cunning plan to humiliate *you*."

"I am beyond humiliation," said Fred. He was getting out his mobile, though. "I am the lowest form of human life. I am totally without style or backbone. Nothing you could possibly do or say could upset me. Stones and grass envy me."

He switched on his mobile and started to text, at speed. Jess tried to take a peek, but Fred shrugged her off. Then he finished his message and pocketed the phone.

"Who were you texting?" demanded Jess, fascinated.

"It's a mystery," said Fred. "Now let's get back to that fire and get some tucker lined up. All that violence has given me an appetite."

They joined Marie-Louise at the campfire, and Edouard also appeared with another armful of logs.

"Isn't he a little treasure?" said Fred.

"Don't talk about him behind his back under his nose like that," said Jess. She was beginning to feel protective towards Edouard. After all, he had rescued her several times that weekend. She smiled at Edouard and he smiled back.

"Good! Wood!" She grinned and gave him the thumbs-up. "Thank you!"

"Goodwood!" said Edouard in a friendly way. "You are a pleasure!" Wow! Communication was taking place. Well, nearly.

Marie-Louise produced a fabulous snack involving Danish pastries, French croissants, and the infamous British treat, the Chelsea bun. They put the kettle on for hot chocolate. Then, suddenly, there was a blast of racing-car noise from Fred's pocket: Fred's Formula One ringtone. He took out his mobile and checked the text message.

"Who is it?" said Jess. "Is it an answer to your SOS?" Fred texted back a few words without answering her. "What's happening?" pleaded Jess.

"I've called in the cavalry," said Fred. "You'll soon find out."

Jess was vastly intrigued, but was obliged to have a long conversation with Marie-Louise about different sorts of dogs, before, eventually, the kettle reached a shrieking boil just as Jodie reappeared.

"Jess," she said, "Auntie Rose says your washing's dry and if you want, you can go and iron it."

"Great!" cried Jess. "Ironing! I so love it! Just the treat I was hoping for." She scrambled to her feet.

"I hear the people who invented skiing holidays are going to market ironing holidays next," said Fred.

"Fabulous! I'll start saving up right now!" said Jess. Despite her hatred of ironing, she was glad to have an excuse to escape from Jodie.

"I'll come with you," said Jodie, disastrously. "Hang on, I'll just get my washing." She grabbed some clothes from the girls' tent and joined Jess. As they turned to go, Jess gave Fred a parting glance. He was pulling his "Jodie angry" face, based on bulging eyes and a sulky, pouting lower lip. Jess almost cracked up, but just managed to restrain herself.

"Right," said Jodie, as they walked to the farmhouse, "so what's the plan?"

"It's going to be a surprise," said Jess.

"Tell me!" ordered Jodie. "Because I've thought of some ace ideas anyway. We could find some frogspawn and fill their sleeping bags with it. Or we could follow them next time they sneak off together for a snog. We could hide in the bushes and make slurping and groaning noises."

"Don't worry," said Jess, secretly appalled at the poverty

of Jodie's imagination—though Jess herself had thought of precisely zilch. "It's all arranged. You don't have to do a thing."

"Yeah, but what *exactly* is going to happen?" said Jodie, nagging away at Jess's side. "It's got to be good, and it's got to be, like, totally, devastatingly *humiliating*. I want Flora *on toast*, OK? So let's have the gory details, right now!"

Jess's mind went into overdrive. What she had hoped would be a relaxing mini-break with the ironing board was going to turn into an interrogation by the Gestapo.

"Look, it's got to be a surprise, right?" Jess was desperately playing for time. Why, oh *why* had she told Jodie that she'd already thought of a devastating trick to play on Flora and Gerard? Bizarrely, it was to try and protect Flora—well, everybody—from Jodie's ferocious temper, which had already nearly caused an international incident.

Ironical, thought Jess. *I've got even more reason to be hacked off with Flora than Jodie has. After all, Gerard's actually hit on me, and I'm damn sure he's never moved in on Jodie, or we'd all know about it by now.*

"It's got to be a surprise to *them*," said Jodie. "It doesn't have to be a surprise to *me*."

"Yeah, but, we decided it would be better if it was a surprise to you, too," said Jess desperately.

"Who's *we*?" demanded Jodie.

"Well, Fred, of course," said Jess as they arrived at the house. "He is a genius, after all."

They went indoors. Jodie's auntie was sitting at the kitchen table, lining up rows and rows of odd socks. Betsy stirred in her basket, barked, grinned, and wagged her tail.

"I'm running a dating agency for single socks," said Auntie Rose. "It's so silly . . . but I can't bear to throw the odd ones away. I feel sort of sad." She sighed. Clearly she was a sentimental old dreamer.

"We do that at home, too," said Jess. "Some socks just want independence and a career."

"Is it OK if I do some laundry?" asked Jodie.

"Of course, yes, yes," said Auntie Rose. "Help yourself." She got up and drifted towards the window. "It's such a lovely day . . ."

Jodie and Jess went through the kitchen to the utility room. Jodie closed the door behind them, and once they'd got the washing machine going there was enough noise to cover their conversation.

"So tell me," said Jodie eagerly, as Jess began to iron her jeans, "what's gonna happen? I can't wait!"

"Guess," said Jess, desperate for suggestions even at this late stage.

"Does it involve cowpats?" asked Jodie.

"Possibly," said Jess. "As the final finishing touch."

"Does it involve mud?" asked Jodie.

"Certainly," said Jess, ironing the legs of her jeans at lightning speed so she could escape from Jodie as soon as possible.

"Does it involve pain?" asked Jodie.

"You bet," said Jess. "Five-star, one hundred percent top-notch, luxury pain."

"And tears, and blood?" asked Jodie eagerly. What a monster she was when roused.

"I can't actually guarantee tears and blood," said Jess. "But you never know your luck."

"What else? Give me a clue," said Jodie, as if this was some kind of Victorian parlor game.

"What else?" Jess's mind drifted, bizarrely, randomly, through the universe. "Black olives," she said thoughtfully. "Mad dogs. A tablespoon of chilli powder. Razor blades. A dead rat dipped in mayo. A dash of lemon juice."

"Ha ha!" Jodie cracked up. "Jess, you are so, like, weird! It's great that you've split up with Flora now. Do you want to come round my house next weekend? We can go bowling and have loads of laughs."

Jess endured a horrid shiver of disgust at the thought of physical exercise—with Jodie, of all people. Jodie was OK, she was fine, she could be fun when not in a strop, but as best mate? Never.

For a moment a short video of Flora flashed through Jess's brain. Beautiful, elegant, clever, giggly Flora. Sensitive, kind Flora. Usually. The video switched into devilish mode and played a little section in which Gerard and Flora strolled down the field, arms wrapped round each other. And then

Flora turned on Jess and gave her a mouthful of venom because Jess dared to criticize her.

"*Bowling?* . . . Er, next weekend's going to be a bit tricky, Jode," said Jess. "Because the Frenchies will still be here, won't they? When are they going home?"

"Oh yeah, Saturday," said Jodie. "Well, maybe the weekend after. Why don't you come round my place? You could stay if you like. Our spare room has got its own TV."

Panic flashed through Jess. She had to escape from Jodie's menacing invites. She so didn't want to replace Flora with Jodie, even if Flora was out of order at the moment.

"Oh, sorry," she said. "My dad's coming up that weekend and I hardly ever see him, so I'll have to stay at home."

"Shame," said Jodie. "We could have celebrated the end of the French invasion. God, how am I going to get through another whole week? I'm not going to speak a word to Gerard. He can talk to my stinking mum. Frankly, I can't wait to see him off."

"Did he ever, you know . . ." Jess hesitated. "Before he got with Flora . . . Did he ever hit on you?"

Jodie hesitated. She frowned. Her lower lip stuck out in the pout so recently parodied by Fred.

"Well, not as such," she admitted. "Not actually—you know. He did give me some looks, though. And when I sent my photo he wrote that I was beautiful." *Another digitally enhanced one, then,* thought Jess, swiftly ironing her T-shirt.

"Did he ever, like, hold your hand or anything?"

"Well." Jodie pursed her lips thoughtfully. "When he arrived he kissed me on both cheeks. And every night at bedtime he kisses me on both cheeks."

"That's hardly wild, raunchy sex," said Jess. "The French kiss each other all the time. Their president even tried to kiss our prime minister last time he visited. I saw it on the news."

"Yeah, yeah, I know," said Jodie. "It's not that I thought Gerard was, like, *mine* or anything. I mean, he's not my *boyfriend*. OK, that's cool. But he is supposed to be my French exchange partner, and since Flora grabbed him he hasn't said a single word to me."

"So you're not jealous, then?" asked Jess.

"Are you kidding? I'm jealous as hell," said Jodie. "I sometimes really hate Flora. I know you and she were best mates, but she really gets up my nose sometimes."

"I never said we weren't best mates anymore," said Jess. "I just think she's out of order right now."

"Well, yeah, whatever," said Jodie. "She deserves what's coming to her."

"Yeah," said Jess hurriedly. "Whatever. I think I've finished now. This fleece doesn't need ironing." She unplugged the iron, grabbed her clean clothes, and headed for the door.

"When's it gonna *happen*?" persisted Jodie, following hard on Jess's heels like a snappy little dog chasing a postman.

"Wait and see!" said Jess with a hint of playful mischief, and slipped through the kitchen. Auntie Rose was staring out of the window.

"Oh, the clouds," she sighed. "Look, girls!" Jodie and Jess glanced obediently out of the window.

"Fabulous," said Jess. "I've never seen clouds like them."

"I'm thinking of taking a photography course," said

Auntie Rose. "I want to specialize in skies. I'm a Libran, you know—it's an air sign."

"Airhead, more like," whispered Jodie as they escaped into the outdoors.

"I think your auntie is a sweetheart," said Jess, eager to turn the conversation away from Flora and Gerard and the terrible revenge that Jess was going to inflict on them, just as soon as she managed to think of it. "I'm sorry she's got that health problem. What is it, exactly?"

"Oh, nothing," said Jodie. "I just made that up because I was so pissed off."

As they rounded the hawthorn hedge, a strange sight met their eyes. A whole crowd of people round the fire! Well, not a whole crowd, really. Flora and Gerard had come back and were sitting all cuddled up, which was, of course, nauseating. However, this was no time for nausea. Because there were new arrivals.

It was a couple of boys from school—guys Jess and Jodie had always rated, although they didn't know them well. One was Mackenzie. He was short, dark, and talkative. He appeared to be trying to wow Marie-Louise with a stream of something resembling French.

It was his mate who was the really big surprise, however: Ben Jones, captain of the school football team. Ben had been absent from school for ages because he'd had acute appendicitis, and it had taken weeks for him to recover. But now he looked in tip-top shape.

He was lounging by the fire, and poking it lazily with a stick. Somehow, he had changed since Jess had last seen him. Maybe it was to do with his hair, which now seemed to have Californian blond highlights. Maybe it was something to do with his legs, which seemed to be much longer than before. *If this is what appendicitis does to people,* thought Jess, *it should be compulsory. Forget the magic potions—go for the pain in the guts.*

"Hi, guys!" called Jodie, swooping down towards them like a ravening wolf approaching a couple of tasty lambs. "Welcome to my auntie's field!"

"It's, like, totally amazing!" said Mackenzie. "If I'd known you were a major landowner, Jode, I'd have hit on you years ago. But hey—I hope it's not too late? Can we get engaged right now?"

Everybody laughed, most of all Jodie. Then she turned to where Ben Jones was lounging in such picturesque style.

"Hey, Ben!" she said. "Are you better and everything? We've really missed you. Will you show us your scar?"

Ben Jones gave her the laziest, sexiest smile and looked slightly embarrassed. Wow! All thoughts of Gerard would soon have vanished from Jodie's head.

"Er . . . well, no, cos it's totally gross," said Ben. He was never one for the verbals. Mackenzie never stopped jabbering, but Ben could hardly ever be bothered to say a word, so in a way Mackenzie was usually talking for two. But right now they were both grinning at Jodie in very powerful sexy stereo.

Jess caught Fred's eye. He raised his eyebrows slightly as if to say, *So what do you think of my cunning plan?* And Jess gave him a satisfied little nod that meant, *Not bad for starters.* The arrival of Ben and Mackenzie had certainly put Jodie back into a good mood. It was a brilliant plan of Fred's—

presumably Ben and Mackenzie were under strict orders to flirt nonstop with Jodie. Now everyone could relax and let the weekend float gently on in a haze of barbecue smoke and bliss.

Or could they? Suddenly Jess felt a raindrop hit her head. The sun had gone in, and Auntie Rose's fabulous clouds were about to dump on them, big-time. There was a distant flash of lightning and a rumble of thunder.

"Oh my God!" shouted Jodie. "Quick! Everyone to the girls' tent!"

It was the only tent big enough to accommodate everybody. *Surely we can't all cram ourselves in there without a huge amount of . . . intimate contact taking place?* thought Jess as she ran towards the tent. She was looking forward to trying.

☆ 34 ☆

*E*verybody piled into the girls' tent, and Jess felt a quick wave of embarrassment at the fact that her PJs were just lying there all crumpled on top of her bag. She grabbed them, stuffed them under her pillow, and sat on it. Marie-Louise tumbled in almost on top of her and the rest of the gang followed: Edouard, Flora and Gerard, then Jodie with Ben Jones and Mackenzie, and finally Fred.

"Make room! Make room!" yelled Fred. "Cyclone approaching! Hailstones the size of golfballs!" There was hardly any room for Fred. He had to stand right by the door. "Shove up!" he said. "My arse is still outdoors! It's going to be struck by lightning!"

"You guys stand up!" said Jodie to Jess, Marie-Louise, and Edouard. "There'll be more room if everybody stands up. This tent wasn't designed for nine."

Jess, Marie-Louise, and Edouard struggled to their feet. In the course of the struggle, Jess spent a dire couple of seconds with her face buried in Marie-Louise's backside, and immediately afterwards received a painful stab in the ribs from Edouard's elbow. It wasn't exactly the kind of intimate contact she had been looking forward to.

Worroworroworroworro! Another thunderclap went hurtling across the sky. Flora screamed and clung on to Gerard. Jodie screamed and clung on to Ben Jones. Less excitingly, Marie-Louise screamed and clung on to Jess. Rain hammered on the roof of the tent. This was not the delightful fairylike touch of a gentle moonlit shower, which can sound so delicious on the tent roof as you lie in your sleeping bag. No, this was weather *war.*

"Maybe we should seek shelter in the house, my friends," said Fred in an old-fashioned voice. " 'Twould be tragic if we were to be struck by lightning and killed. Well, 'twould be tragic if I perished, anyway."

"*No!*" said Jodie. "We're much better off where we are!"

She was certainly better off where she was—with Ben Jones's arms around her. His expression wasn't exactly ecstatic, though. You could never quite tell what Ben was thinking, but it was obvious that if he really wanted, he could do much better than cuddling up to Jodie.

Eventually, after a few more rumbles of thunder and much synchronized screaming, the rain eased off and the thunder seemed to roll away into the distance. They stepped out into the saturated field. The dark cloud was scudding off towards the horizon. Sun now poured down and the grass actually steamed.

"Oh my God!" cried Flora. "A rainbow!"

There it was, cutely poised over Auntie Rosie's house. Moments later, Auntie Rosie ran into view, clutching her camera. She aimed it at the sky and fired. Then she turned back and waved.

"Everybody OK?" she called. "Nobody drowned or struck by lightning?"

"All OK!" yelled Jodie. And then added in a kind of whisper, "Oh my God! Remember she said there were only supposed to be six of us! Quick, let's go down to the river."

Everybody took off at speed, with Jess and Fred bringing up the rear. Jess hated sport and never worked out: Fred was just a feeble swot.

"And the plucky English girl is fading fast!" puffed Fred in his sports-commentator voice. "The French are in the lead! They're going to get gold and silver! The British team is absolutely nowhere!"

Fred's account of things was not quite true. Ben Jones seemed to have won the race down to the river, and Gerard was second. Edouard came in third, because his legs were shorter.

"Hey! Why don't we have a picnic lunch down here?" said Flora.

"But it is wet, ze grass!" objected Marie-Louise, looking down in horror at the glistening earth.

"We could get a blanket or something," said Jodie

thoughtfully. "Maybe Auntie's got a sort of tarpaulin thing. I've seen them in the barn."

Suddenly, Jess felt a raindrop hit her nose. Oh no! Another shower! Before anyone could decide what to do about it, another fierce little storm blew up. There was no thunder or lightning this time, just rain, and plenty of it. At first everyone sheltered under a tree, but then the tree itself started to drip. Flora got the giggles.

"Oh, what the hell!" she cried, and waltzed out onto the open grass. She looked up to the heavens, stretched out her arms, and laughed. "Rain on me as much as you like!" she yelled. Rain ran down her face. She laughed and sort of danced about, getting wetter and wetter. "If you can't beat it, join it!" she cried.

"Flora Barclay of Ashcroft Harriers seems to have taken leave of her senses," said Fred in his commentator's voice. "They're sending in the St. John's Ambulance people now, and I suspect they may be escorting her along to the nearby Fred Parsons Memorial Psychiatric Unit."

Gerard joined Flora in the field, and they held hands and whirled around at speed.

"Zey are a bit stupide," said Marie-Louise quietly. She was still clinging to the tree trunk, trying to shelter, and casting longing glances up the hill to the tents, or even better, the farmhouse.

"So, Ben, when are you coming back to school?" asked Jodie, grinning eagerly. The sight of Flora and Gerard dancing in the rain didn't seem to have upset her one little bit.

"Yeah . . . on Monday," said Ben. His voice was divine: growly and somehow golden.

The rain stopped and the sun came out, possibly as a result of Ben Jones having spoken. Everybody was a little damp, but Flora and Gerard were absolutely saturated.

The group relaxed a little, and moved away from the tree. It was too wet to sit down, so they just stood about. Ben Jones caught hold of the ropes that were hanging from the branch of the tree, above the river. He disentangled them.

Ben tested them, selected one, took hold of it carefully, and with a great push, launched himself across the river. He didn't drop down on the other side—he just swung to and fro. Everybody watched. All the girls were mesmerized. Even Flora stopped dancing about with Gerard and stared in admiration at Ben for a while.

Then, all of a sudden, Gerard grabbed the other rope and also started swinging to and fro. He raised his feet and next time he swung past Ben, he gave him a friendly but firm push. It didn't seem to affect Ben at all, but it threw Gerard totally out of line. Gerard's rope sort of whirled round and round, out of its usual pattern, and came back, heading for a big collision with Ben.

"Feet up!" yelled Mackenzie from the bank. They both raised their feet and collided—or at least, their trainers did. Gerard's rope went whirling around again, out of control. Now Ben's rope was swinging in a dangerous random way, too.

"And the French have lost it," said Fred in his commentator's voice. "That was almost a foul. I wouldn't be surprised if he got a yellow card for that, or possibly a penalty point and one hand cut off for cheating."

Gerard and Ben swung towards each other again, and this

time Gerard, rather stupidly, gave one hell of a heave with his feet—so much, in fact, that he lost his grip on the rope, swore (in French), and started to fall. The girls screamed. Everything seemed to go into slow motion.

Jess hoped he wasn't going to fall in the river or hit his head. Thank God he landed on the bank, on his feet. But he hit the ground awkwardly, at an angle: his ankle buckled under him and he fell heavily on his side, letting out a terrible howl. He grabbed his ankle and kept yelling, "Ma cheville! Ma cheville!" And he went a truly horrible shade of green.

Flora flew to his side, knelt down beside him, and panicked in a really irritating way, like somebody in a silent movie. She stroked his head, she tried to hold his hand, she touched his leg, she generally made herself totally useless.

"What shall we do?" she shouted. "What shall we do? What shall we do?"

"Fetch Auntie Rose, somebody!" said Jodie, also kneeling down by Gerard. Marie-Louise ran a few steps uphill, then came back.

"I cannot speak ze English enough good!" she said.

"Ben!" shouted Jodie. "Run!" Ben set off. "No, wait, come back!" yelled Jodie. "You don't even know Auntie Rose. You don't know where the kitchen is or anything. Fred, you go." Fred shrugged, looked useless, and set off. Ben came back and squatted down by Gerard.

"It could be broken, it could be just sprained," said Mackenzie. "Give the guy time."

"Sorry, mate," said Ben, looking at Gerard with true concern. Gerard ignored him.

Jess watched the whole event in a kind of freeze-frame.

What if Gerard had broken his ankle? How totally, utterly awful. And what if the pain was so bad, he was sick? His face was that horrible green color. Jess hoped that, even if he had broken his ankle, Gerard would have the heroic self-control not to be sick. But Gerard did something worse. He *cried*.

It was embarrassing. Flora grabbed his hand and stroked it, but he pushed her away. Marie-Louise fussed about, getting out her hankie but feeling too embarrassed to offer it. Edouard hovered nearby, just in case a healing insect might be required. Ben Jones stayed right beside Gerard, with one hand on his shoulder. Mackenzie just gabbled.

"I'm sure it's not broken, cos we'd have heard the crack. Did anybody hear a crack? I didn't hear a crack."

After what seemed like a century, Auntie Rose came hurtling down the field, with Fred following. He was far too cool to be seen running, especially in the company of a middle-aged woman carrying a shopping bag.

Auntie Rose arrived, examined Gerard's ankle, spoke to him quietly in French, rummaged about in her bag, and produced a pack of frozen peas, which she slapped on his foot.

"That should stop the swelling," she said. "I've rung Geoff on his mobile and asked him to come down here with the four-wheel-drive. He'll be down in a few minutes. I don't think it's broken, but maybe we should take him to the accident and emergency unit, just in case. Geoff will know what to do. The animals are always hurting themselves."

"It's a good job he's not a racehorse," said Fred. "Or he might have to be shot."

"Shut up, Fred!" snapped Jess. When not being totally brilliant, Fred was the biggest idiot in the world.

odie's uncle Geoff turned up in a 4x4, liberally gar-
nished with cow poo. He was a huge guy, covered
in straw and looking a bit annoyed. He and Aunt
Rose helped Gerard into the back (still holding the pack of
frozen peas on his ankle) and drove him up to the house.
The rest of the gang trudged back up the field. It was raining again.

"Oh God, I hope Gerard hasn't broken his ankle!"
said Flora.

"Course he hasn't," said Jodie. "He's just making a fuss.
He's such a crybaby."

"Rather harsh," said Jess. "I frequently cry at adverts for

old-fashioned bread, especially if they involve grandpas. And you only have to say 'kittens' to Flora and she's off."

"Yes, but he's a bloke," said Jodie. "Guys are supposed to be strong and manly and stuff. I could never fancy a bloke who cried when he sprained his ankle. I went right off him."

"Really?" said Flora coldly. "It only made me like him more."

They walked on in silence until they reached the tents. Fred and Edouard climbed into the boys' tent. Ben Jones and Mackenzie walked off to where they had left their mountain bikes under a tree, and got out their jackets. The girls went into their tent to try and find dry clothes. Jodie looked grumpy and martyred.

"I suppose I'd better get up to the house and sit by his side and hold his goddamn hand," she said, with just the faintest hint of grim triumph. Flora, who was drying her hair, stopped suddenly, fiddled with her rings, and looked at the ground.

"Could I come, too?" she asked timidly. Jess hated her for this. Why couldn't she just keep her dignity intact? Why did she have to beg Jodie for another chance to drool all over Gerard?

"The thing is," said Jodie, with a furtive look on her face, like a politician who is lying at a press conference, "I'm beginning to think we should cancel the weekend and go home. All this rain and stuff. We're all soaked. Especially you." She glared at Flora, who was still saturated from her Mad Dance of Love in the rain. Flora blushed slightly.

"Yeah, well . . . ," Flora said, shrugging and trying unsuccessfully to look as if it was all the same to her whether she ever saw Gerard again. "My dad did send me a text saying they'd changed the weather forecast and the rain's going to come back and get worse."

"It is stinking cold as well," said Jess, pulling on an extra fleece. This camping business had turned a little sour.

"I'd better go and see how he is," said Jodie.

"I'll come, too—just for a minute," said Flora.

"Knock, knock!" said a voice outside the tent. It was Mackenzie. Ben Jones was standing behind him, looking dreamily down towards the river as if he didn't really mind if he saw any of the girls or not. "We're going now," said Mackenzie. "Cos it's all gone pear-shaped with all this rain and people's legs hanging off and stuff."

"Whatever," said Jodie. "See you on Monday—and don't forget, Ben, you're going to show us your scar!" She reached out and gave the waistband of his trousers a playful little pull. God, she was such a shameless tart in her bull-dozing way!

Ben Jones looked startled and embarrassed, but managed a rueful smile. Just for a split second Jess caught his eye, and they exchanged a psychic message. *Sorry Jodie is such a slapper,* was Jess's mental message. *Don't worry, she doesn't bother me,* replied Ben telepathically. *You're the one who intrigues me. I want to be alone with you. I want to stare deep into your magnificent eyes. I want to hold your hand for a century. I want to be your partner in Britain's Olympic kissing team.*

Well, that was what he said in Jess's imagination, anyway. The New Improved Ben Jones was really über-gorgeous. When he'd been lounging about by the fire he'd looked like

Brad Pitt's kid brother in a cowboy movie. When he'd run off down the river and got there first he'd looked like David Beckham's kid brother in a European Cup Final. And when he'd swung about on that rope it had been Tarzan Returns. *You Tarzan—me Jess* . . . Jess sighed. He looked away again.

Jodie and Flora went off to the farmhouse, and Ben Jones and Mackenzie said goodbye and strolled off to collect their bikes. Jess admired Ben's back. His bum was five-star perfection. Mackenzie, though short, was kind of cute, but he just wasn't in the frame. Flora had said once she thought he looked a bit like Elijah Wood. But right now, Jess had eyes for nobody but Ben, and Flora had eyes for nobody but Gerard.

Jess zipped up her fleece and stepped back inside the girls' tent. Marie-Louise was packing. She looked up.

"We are goingue 'ome, yes?" she inquired.

"I think so," sighed Jess. "It's all gone pear-shaped."

"Excuse me?" Marie-Louise frowned slightly. Jess sighed again.

"Sorry," she said. "Just an English phrase. Time to call it a day." Marie-Louise frowned again. "Oh, sorry," said Jess. "Another English phrase. Er . . . how about: the party's over?"

"Ah!" smiled Marie-Louise. "I h'understand." She went back to her packing. She was doing it immaculately, rolling up items of clothing and smoothing them down in her dinky little bag. She looked as if she was really enjoying herself.

"I'd better go and tell Fred and Edouard," said Jess. She

stepped out of the tent and sighed again. The image of Ben Jones appeared in her mind's eye, surrounded by shimmering light and hovering slightly above the ground. Supernatural rays played around his golden head and he seemed to smile mysteriously while beckoning her to some divine destination, preferably adorned with palm trees.

"Oh, cut it out, for God's sake!" she said to herself, aloud. "He may be well fit but he's not the actual Son of God. Control yourself, woman!" Obediently she stopped thinking about Ben Jones. But she sort of stashed him away in a secret corner of her mind, and she was looking forward to revisiting that sacred corner in the very near future.

Fred stepped out of the boys' tent, carrying his Stephen King book, which was the size of a brick.

"So what's next in this endless round of pleasure?" he asked, tucking his book inside his jacket to shelter it from the rain. "Did I hear a barn mentioned? Shall we adjourn there? Would you like me to read you deeply disturbing extracts from my book until you go screamingly insane?"

"Normally I'd jump at the chance," said Jess. "But apparently the show's over, and we've all got to pack. Jodie's decided, what with Gerard's ankle and the rain and everything."

"Well, thank God for that," said Fred. "I thought the torture would never end."

"I'll just tell Edouard to pack up his spiders and get ready to roll," said Jess. She stepped inside the boys' tent, which predictably smelt of pongy socks. Edouard was sitting on his neatly folded sleeping bag, playing with his Game Boy.

"We go home now," said Jess, speaking, for some reason, like an Indian guide in an old-style Western. "Rain. No good. Go home today. Now. I ring mother." She got her phone out.

Amazingly, Edouard seemed to understand. He switched off his Game Boy and started to pack. Jess called her mum.

"Thank God you rang!" said Mum. "I was getting really worried. Are you all right?"

"I'm all right, but Gerard's done something to his ankle," said Jess.

"Oh no!" gasped Mum in horror. "I knew it! I just knew it! Whatever will I say to his parents?"

"Gerard, not Edouard," said Jess. "Calm down, for God's sake, Mum."

"Sorry, sorry," said Mum. "I lost it for a moment there, because they both end in 'ard.'"

Jess could see that there was a joke tucked away in there somewhere, but she didn't have time for it right now.

"OK, but listen," said Jess. "Can you come and collect us? Like, now? Because apparently this rain's going to get worse." Fred loomed up beside Jess and started to perform a charade. "Oh—and can we give Fred a lift home?"

"Of course, of course, I'll come right away," said Mum. "I'll be there in half an hour." She rang off, sounding hugely relieved, as if she'd been imagining Jess being chased by cattle, falling in the river, and having her heart broken a hundred different ways.

Come to think of it, something very similar had indeed happened, but it didn't seem to matter now.

"I just hate the way Jodie throws herself at Ben," Jess said, putting her phone away. "If you were a guy—and you sort of are—wouldn't it put you right off?"

"Oh, certainly," said Fred. "I'd run like hell."

"I'd rather be an eccentric old spinster than hurl myself at boys the way Jodie and Flora do," said Jess.

"Just as well," said Fred. "As you're clearly destined to be an eccentric old spinster anyway. I mean, who'd have you?"

Jess pulled Fred's hair and punched him playfully in the ribs. He gave her a Chinese burn. Edouard looked up from his packing in alarm, then realized it was only a joke.

"Anyway," said Jess, "I'll leave you to do your stuff. Get a move on. My mum will be here in thirty."

"It'll only take me two seconds to pack," said Fred. "What else is there to do?"

"I believe this is your tent?" said Jess tauntingly. "Someone has to take it down . . . ? And fold it up nice and tidily so it fits in the back of my mum's car . . . ?" Fred went pale.

"Oh Lawdy," he said. "Help me, please!"

"Sorry," said Jess. "Stuff to do!" And she ducked out of the tent and skipped off through the rain towards the loo. Before she got there Jodie came barging down the path.

"We're taking Gerard to A and E as a precaution!" she said importantly. "For an X-ray, you know . . . Flora's just snogging him goodbye. She'll be here in a min— I just wanted to say . . ." Jodie leant in towards Jess and dropped her voice to a whisper—well, by Jodie's standards, anyway. ". . . Congrats on your utterly brilliant revenge! Water, mud, five-star pain: it was all there, exactly as promised!"

Then she abruptly stopped as Flora appeared, coming down the path and talking on her mobile. Jess was amazed. Did Jodie actually think she and Fred had cooked up Gerard's accident? If so, she must be quite extraordinarily stupid.

"Gotta go!" said Jodie, turning back towards the house. "The weekend is canceled! See you on Monday!"

Jodie went back up the path, passing Flora and ignoring her. You could tell just by looking at Jodie's back that she was utterly triumphant. The way she brushed past Flora said, *Gerard's mine now—mine to take to hospital, mine to take home and look after . . . But d'you know what? I couldn't care less anyway. He's rubbish, because now I'm fixated on Ben Jones's appendectomy scar!*

Flora arrived where Jess was standing, and quickly finished her phone call.

"OK, see you in half an hour, then, Mum—thanks!—Yes, Marie-Louise is fine!" Flora put her phone in her pocket and stood, looking sorrowfully at Jess. Tears filled her eyes.

"So, Jess," she said with a rather tense, unhappy smile, "are we friends, or not?"

"I can't think about anything else until I've been to the loo," said Jess, and walked away. As she sat in the peace and quiet of the outdoor lavatory, she wondered if perhaps she had been a teensy bit harsh to Flora.

On second thoughts, perhaps, no.

"Of course we're still friends," said Jess as they walked back down towards the campfire together. But she didn't manage to say it in that bouncy, sincere, adoring way she might have managed last week.

It wasn't just that Flora had gone off with Gerard after he had seemed to be interested in Jess. After all, Flora hadn't known he'd held Jess's hand or said those things. It was more to do with the way Flora had acted once she and Gerard were an item: as if Jess hardly existed.

Once she and Gerard had tasted the delights of snogging in the open air, Flora had barely exchanged a word with

Jess. She'd only whispered to her at night to report details of her heavenly evening. And she'd only returned to the campfire to steal a mighty portion of Jess's breakfast—after publicly announcing that she wasn't hungry.

That last act of carefree greediness was almost the worst thing of all. Stealing someone's guy was, well, sometimes unavoidable, maybe; stealing someone's breakfast was a capital offense. At least in Jess's eyes.

It just seemed to sum up Flora's character. She was greedy. It wasn't her fault. She just assumed that she was entitled to things: other people's French exchange partners, other people's scrambled egg. She was like a swarm of gorgeous golden locusts.

"Oh, I'm so glad!" Flora squeezed Jess's arm. "We're best mates, then, like always?"

"Why wouldn't we be?" said Jess, with a shrug. But there was definitely something tetchy in the air. Jess was quite enjoying it, actually. Watching Flora squirm was almost the best moment of the weekend so far.

"Well, it's like . . . I don't feel I've seen very much of you the past couple of days," said Flora.

"Well, whose fault is that?" said Jess. "You've been otherwise engaged."

"I'm sorry," said Flora guiltily. "I'm really sorry, Jess. But Gerard's going home in a few days and we've got to make the most of our time together. I might not see him again for months."

"So what's the plan?" asked Jess. "Getting engaged at Christmas, are we?"

"Oh, don't be stupid, Jess. Of course not!" laughed Flora

in an anxious, slippery way. It was just as if that very thought was festering in her golden glamorous mind. "It's way too soon for anything like that."

Way too soon, eh? thought Jess. A revealing phrase. It showed Flora was thinking big. Jess could almost hear wedding bells—in French.

"Besides," Flora went on, "I'll have to be really tactful from now on, because Jodie's got it in for me. Stick up for me, won't you, Jess? She's not even speaking to me at the moment. Like I've committed some horrible crime or something."

They arrived at the campfire, which was fizzling damply. Marie-Louise was packing up all the plastic boxes and cooking equipment, trying to remember which boxes belonged to which family. Flora immediately knelt down and started to help her. Fred and Edouard were taking down the boys' tent, badly, and swearing bilingually in stereo. The campsite looked sad and finished.

Jess's mum was the first parent to arrive. As usual she was wearing dire old Oxfam clothes, but as it was raining steadily by now, nobody noticed. Jess, Edouard, and Fred piled into Mum's ancient estate car, along with the tent and all the sleeping bags.

"So, how did it go?" asked Mum as they set off down the farm track.

"Oh, fabulous," said Jess. That was enough info, in her view.

"Fabulous?" said Mum. "With poor what's-his-name breaking his ankle, and thunderstorms?"

"Oh, terrible, then," said Jess. She was getting quite high

on being back in the car. She was beginning to feel dry and warm and indoorish, and realized how much she had missed it.

"What did you think of it, Fred?" asked Mum.

"Well, I'm not really the sporty outdoor type," said Fred. "I prefer to fester on the sofa, watching TV and eating chips. Personally, the rain couldn't come too soon."

"You did enjoy the charades, though, admit it," said Jess.

"Charades?" said Mum, sounding pleased because she thought charades would have been unsexy.

"Oh yes," said Fred. "The bingo was also excellent. And the Bible-reading."

Jess smiled dreamily, but Fred's words drifted lazily around the outside of her mind. Secretly she was revisiting the sacred part of her memory banks where Ben Jones lay, folded up and waiting. Gingerly she approached the magic jewel-studded chest. She lifted the lid . . .

Out sprang Ben Jones, rather delightfully wearing football shorts, which was thoughtful of him. He trotted round the circuit of Jess's mind for a few seconds and then swept her up in his arms and carried her, giggling, to a red velvet couch, where . . .

"Are you hungry?" asked Mum, from several hundred miles away.

"When am I not hungry?" said Jess automatically. Although, curiously, she was not quite as hungry as usual. It was ages since breakfast, and Flora had stolen half of that. But every time she thought of Ben Jones, Jess got a peculiar and delicious feeling in her tum that was even more enjoyable than devouring eggs and bacon.

They dropped Fred off at his house and stopped for fish and chips on the way home.

"After all, it is an English thing," said Jess. "Edouard likes chips, too."

"I suppose," sighed Mum. "It is part of our culture, after all."

They sat in the car eating fish and chips out of newspaper as it was more fun and more English than taking them home. The rain continued to fall. The windows steamed up.

"So, Mum," said Jess. "What's happened in the rest of the world?"

"There's been a bomb blast in the Middle East," said Mum, sounding worried. Instantly Jess rejoined Ben Jones on the red velvet sofa. He wrapped his arms around her and they stared into each other's eyes.

"God, you're beautiful," said Ben Jones, in a faint American accent, sounding a bit like Brad Pitt.

"And there's a crisis about tax," added Mum. "Because of the budget."

"I'm filming a comedy thriller in Hollywood, starting Monday," Ben went on, stroking Jess's hair, which was suddenly, mysteriously, long and blond. "I want you to come with me. I've rented a beach house in Malibu. It has a maid, a chauffeur, a butler, and complimentary matching dogs."

"And I took Granny back home yesterday," said Mum. "She's fine now. She's come to her senses. I'm absolutely shattered, though. I shall have to have a lie down as soon as we get home."

"You're my soul mate," sighed Ben, and his lips moved nearer and nearer to hers . . .

"You haven't eaten all your chips, Jess," said Mum with concern, finishing her own meal and putting the rubbish in a convenient in-car bag. "I hope you're not sickening for something."

"Oh, no, no, I'm just a bit tired," said Jess, hastily forcing down another long, limp, glistening masterpiece. "I didn't sleep very well last night. Marie-Louise snored. In French. Although, in a way, I think everybody snores in French."

"Don't say anything racist, just in case," said Mum.

"Don't you mean, don't say anything racist cos it's wrong?" said Jess.

"Of course, of course," said Mum, wiping her hands on her coat (she was that sort of mother) and starting the car. "Did the Queen enjoy her outing?"

"Ask her yourself," said Jess. "I know you're dying to practice a bit more of your flawless French."

Mum said something in French to Edouard, who replied. They talked for some minutes. This was restful. Jess rejoined Ben Jones at their Malibu beach home and had the best fun, running up and down the beach with the matching dogs—who were wearing cute Lycra doggie beach shorts.

"Edouard seems to have enjoyed himself quite a lot." Mum cruelly cut into Jess's daydream again. "He seems to have come out of his shell a bit. I think it did him the world of good."

Jess was quite startled by the idea that Edouard had enjoyed himself. In a way she had hardly been aware he'd been there. Her mind had been so full of Flora and Gerard and Jodie and Ben Jones, she hadn't really given Edouard a thought. But all the time he'd been there, having his own little weekend in his own little life. And he'd enjoyed it! How sweet!

"He rescued me from a whole series of disasters," said Jess, suddenly remembering that, though she had barely been aware of Edouard's presence, she had shamelessly exploited his good nature and camping skills. "We got lost on a walk and he pulled me out of a river, and then I scratched myself on a bit of rusty wire and he sucked the poison out."

"What a hero," said Mum. "He's got hidden depths."

"And then he really came up with the goods and got rid of a spider that was in our tent," said Jess.

No wonder Edouard had enjoyed himself. Jess suddenly realized he had starred in a series of rescue roles. However, as he was small and strange, she had hardly even noticed. She was grateful, though, truly grateful.

So grateful that when they got home and he disappeared up to his room, she almost felt sorry and hoped he was not lonely. However, moments later he came down carrying a CD case. He stood in front of Jess like a cute little soldier on a parade and said, "Jess—will you like playing my computer game?"

My God! He was talking to her! Jess seized the opportunity for endless hours at the PC, especially as her mum was crawling off to bed for one of her tragic headachy little sleeps.

❋ 37 ❋

English hand →

"Bag o' sweets"

← French arm

= HARMONY

"Flora is such a bitch," Jodie whispered. It was back to school with a vengeance, and poisonous gossip was still a dish to be savored. Flora was sitting on a distant wall with Gerard, nuzzling and giggling. Jodie and Jess were eating their baguettes on the bench in the science quad.

"I almost wish lover boy *had* broken his stinking ankle!" Jodie went on, through a mouthful of chicken tikka. Gerard's sacred ankle had, in fact, only been sprained. He had merely acquired a glamorous limp.

"Anyway, who cares?" said Jodie. "My next mission is to get to see Ben Jones's appendectomy scar. I'm going to take a photo of it with my mobile and use it as my screensaver."

"You are one sad sicko," said Jess.

Two girls came up—the ones they'd turfed off this bench a few weeks ago. What were their names again?

"Hi!" said the dark-haired spotty one. "Zoe and Chloe—remember? Your fan base, such as it is. Thought of any good jokes lately?"

"How about a picture of an appendectomy scar as a screensaver?" said Jodie.

"That's not funny, that's gross!" screamed Chloe.

"I wonder what they've done with his appendix," mused Jess.

"Whose appendix?" asked Zoe.

"Ben Jones's."

Zoe and Chloe made appropriate fainting-with-pleasure faces at the mention of the divine name.

"It seems such a waste," Jess went on, "just chucking it in the hospital incinerator. I would have given it a good home. I could have kept it in a little box, like a pet." Zoe and Chloe cracked up.

"Or possibly," Jess continued, "I would have made it into a chic pâté and eaten it on toast. It would be almost like having his baby." Zoe and Chloe shrieked.

"I would have made it into a hairslide," said Jodie. Zoe and Chloe laughed politely.

"Anyway, listen," said Chloe. "Will you sponsor us? We're doing a marathon chess tournament."

"No," said Jodie. "I'm broke. Push off."

"Don't be so harsh, Jode," said Jess. "You're turning into a grouchy old ogre."

"It's in aid of the Teenage Cancer Trust," said Zoe, looking hopeful.

"OK," said Jess. "Put me down for a couple of pounds. I'll catch you later, OK? But you'll never get any money off Jodie. She's a professional skinflint."

Zoe and Chloe departed and the bell rang for afternoon school. Flora tore herself from Gerard's side, came over to Jess, and took her arm. Jodie marched off, looking evil.

"Jodie is such a bad-tempered cow," whispered Flora as they strolled to history. "Gerard said she's really moody with him at home and everything. I mean, it's not his fault we got together. It just sort of happened. You know how it is when you just get swept off your feet—you know, you get these feelings, and they just blow you away, yeah?"

"I wouldn't know," said Jess. She was thinking of the feelings she'd had when Gerard had held her hand underwater, and how easily she could have been blown away by them.

"I wish you wouldn't spend so much time with Jodie," said Flora. "I sometimes think she's trying to turn you against me."

"I have no alternative," said Jess. "My best mate is otherwise engaged, and so is Jodie's French exchange partner."

"It's only till the end of the week," pleaded Flora. "I'm really sorry if I'm neglecting you, Jess. But Gerard goes home on Saturday and I don't know when I'll see him again." She paused. "Or even, well—if I'll *ever* see him again." She gave one of her tragic sniffs. "Don't be mad at me. It's just—you know, well, I hope one day you'll have an experience like this. I hope you'll feel the same kind of thing I feel when I'm with Gerard."

"No, thanks!" said Jess with a mock shudder. "I'm going to be a glamorous spinster like Miss Marple, with some knitting and a nose for homicide."

She could hardly tell Flora that she already *had* felt the same kind of thing that Flora felt when she was with Gerard—and, what a coincidence! She'd felt it *with* Gerard, too.

"Jess, I majorly adore you," whispered Flora as they neared the history room. "You are so great, you're so funny. Always be my friend and look after me. Promise. Because I'm such a feeble dimwit."

Thus spoke Jess's beautiful best buddy, with her straight As, who was dating the only guy who had ever held Jess's hand underwater and made Jess's heart turn somersaults. But in a way, what Flora said about herself was kind of true. Despite all her accomplishments, there was something really vulnerable about Flora. This was touching, if inconvenient.

Jess found it really hard to bear Flora's starstruck confidences about Gerard. But no way could she hurt Flora's feelings and destroy her happiness by telling her that Gerard had hit on her, too—and only minutes before he'd hit on Flora.

Ah, what the hell, it's all history, thought Jess, appropriately entering the history room. All the same, she felt emotionally drained. And to make it worse, Fred was away with a cold. He was *such* a wimp.

What with Jodie pouring anti-Flora poison into her right ear, and Flora pouring anti-Jodie propaganda into her left ear, Jess's head was ringing.

She was actually looking forward to the walk home with Edouard. It would take place in a friendly silence, punctuated only by the offer of sweets.

They were getting along OK these days, Jess and Edouard. They had a "relationship" that revolved around sharing little food treats, playing computer games, and never, under any circumstances, attempting to communicate either in French or English. This could be the start of something small.

38

Au Revoir! Adieu! Goodbye!

aturday morning finally came. The French party was due to leave. Edouard came downstairs, trying to hide his relief and carrying two tiny presents gift-wrapped in silver paper. He placed one by Mum's plate and gave the other to Jess.

Jess's mouth was full of toast and marmalade.

"Mmmmmmf—waugh—hmmmmm—mmmmm—ankoo very much!" she spluttered. Carefully she undid the wrapping paper. Edouard watched, embarrassed.

A small box was revealed, containing a pair of utterly gorgeous treble-hooped earrings. Edouard looked as if he had never seen them before.

"At a guess it was the Queen's mother who is responsible for this delightful gesture," said Mum, opening her present also. A tiny pair of pearl earrings was revealed. Mum whooped with exaggerated joy.

"Well, you'd be worried by any guy who would buy and gift-wrap earrings for women he'd never met," said Jess. "Not counting Elton John and Co, of course."

They put on their new earrings and admired themselves in the mirror.

"Crone with a Pearl Earring," said Mum, fishing for compliments as usual.

"Porn Queen Sporting Fabulous Bling," said Jess, pouting hideously at her reflection.

They both kissed Edouard, which he endured heroically, and shortly afterwards it was time to leave. Jess had a feeling that he had been packed and ready for days. So much for him having a crush on her. (*Thank God!*)

The car park of the leisure center was crowded with cars. French English teachers, English French teachers, and students were all embracing each other, some with genuine affection.

"Thank you for your hospital," said Edouard solemnly. They exchanged awkward, formal kisses. Over Edouard's shoulder, Jess could see Flora and Gerard, wrapped in a tragic final snog.

Edouard was first onto the bus. It was clear he had no wish to linger. But once installed in a window seat, he seemed overcome with last-minute tenderness. He blew kisses at Jess and Mum and waved in a frenzied manner, as if he loved them best in all the world.

"He looks really happy," said Jess. "Do you think he enjoyed himself just a tiny little bit?"

"I shouldn't think so for a moment," said Mum. "He's just overjoyed at the thought that he'll never have to speak to us, ever again."

"What about when I go and stay with him next year?" groaned Jess.

"Oh yes, I was forgetting," said Mum. "Of course. Next it'll be your turn to experience the endless torture of homesickness and strange food. There is no animal so horrid that the French will not attempt to eat it."

"Donkeys, hippos, meerkats—wheel 'em on, kebabbed," said Jess. Though secretly she was planning to develop appendicitis next year. Her French trip would have to be canceled, and Ben Jones would stop in the corridor and say, "I hear you've had appendicitis. How's the scar? I'll show you mine if you show me yours."

"Jess!" a voice jolted her out of her daydream. It was Marie-Louise, who kissed her goodbye with such ferocity that her cheeks hurt. Marie-Louise handed Jess her card with her address on it, and Jess promised to stay in touch.

Then somebody tapped her on the shoulder. She turned round. It was Gerard. His green eyes were fixed on her. He grabbed both her hands and kissed her: left, right, left. Jess couldn't help feeling a little tiny flutter, just for old times' sake.

Then he swept her into his arms for a goodbye hug. He smelt really nice. Jess tried not to enjoy it too much. She knew that Flora, and possibly Jodie, would be watching and that, though tempted to cling on slightly, she must, in fact, let go.

But a split second before releasing her, Gerard whispered something in her ear.

"Jess . . . lovely Jess! I would like to kiss you all over. Please, write to me."

Jess was thunderstruck.

Then he let her go and presented her with his card. Off he went, hugging and kissing the others and giving everybody his card. Was he whispering that kind of stuff to everybody? Jess stood still, totally gobsmacked, in a freeze frame. *What had he said, again? I would like to kiss you all over?* All over?! The filthy swine! The treacherous bastard!

Maybe she had misheard. Surely he hadn't said that? Maybe he had said, *I'll miss you but I'm glad it's all over?* She was utterly speechless, amazed, shocked, and stunned. She just wanted to be somewhere else, and fast.

"Come on, Mum," she said. "Let's go."

"Wait a minute," said Mum. "We have to see them off."

The rest of the goodbyes passed in a blur, but eventually the French buses swept away out of the car park, leaving an unpleasant smell of carbon monoxide.

"Well," said Mum, with a relieved sigh, "that's the end of that little saga."

But it wasn't, quite.

39

Ben Jones

*N*ext day Jess and Flora went to the ice rink, but Flora was in low spirits.

"I miss him *so* much," she said, her blue eyes huge and glistening with tears as they glided round the gloomy cavernous rink to the sound of terrible 1980s music.

Jess said nothing. She couldn't tell Flora about what Gerard had said about wanting to kiss her, etc. It would devastate her. Jess just gritted her teeth and concentrated on not falling on her bum.

"He sent me five texts yesterday, when he was on the journey home," said Flora.

"Terrific," said Jess. "Must be some kind of record." It was really hard not to take the piss.

"But nothing today," said Flora.

"Well, he's probably asleep after the journey," said Jess.

"Time is meaningless," sighed Flora. "It seems about a month since yesterday. I'm going to e-mail him as soon as I get home."

Monday arrived: back to normal school. For Jess life now revolved around trying to get a glimpse of Ben Jones. He wasn't in their class, but there was always the chance of seeing him strolling around the corridors somewhere.

Jess started to keep a BenLog in the back of her rough book. It went like this:

Mon 11.30 a.m. Suspect spotted outside art room. Only back view available. Heart leapt into mouth, though, and stomach tied itself in cute but pulsating bow.

Mon 2 p.m. Suspect spotted in distance on school field, practicing football. Took up position on low wall by rosebeds. Damn, no binoculars. Heart thudded wildly for twenty minutes, like the hooves of a stampeding buffalo.

Mon 4 p.m. Somebody resembling suspect seen by school gate. Turned out to be Toby Williams. Same height, same blond hair, but when he turned round, face like a meat pie. Howled at the moon like a lovesick wolf.

Jess walked home with Flora, quite pleased with her day's work. Two sightings of Ben Jones wasn't bad for starters, though eventually, of course, she hoped to actually bump into him instead of casting longing looks at his arse disappearing in the distance.

One day—possibly tomorrow?—there might be an actual encounter in a corridor. He would smile. He would say, "Hi, Jess." He would throw his arms around her and whisper, "I've been praying I would bump into you outside geography."

"He hasn't e-mailed me," said Flora in a voice of anguish, breaking into Jess's divine fantasy. "And he still hasn't texted me since Sunday night."

"Cheer up!" said Jess. "I'm sure he will."

The week passed agonizingly slowly for Flora, but for Jess the days were full of excitement. Thursday at 2:30 p.m. was Jess's personal high point.

Face to face with Ben Jones outside staffroom! He was talking to sports teacher Mr. Monroe. But he grinned at me. Heart flew out of my mouth, was punted 40 meters across field by Beckham, then headed by Rooney into the back of the net. Result! Heart now back inside body but covered with mud and throbbing strangely. N.B. Must try and get interested in football.

Friday was the last day of school before the Easter hols. Everybody was overjoyed. But for once, Jess would gladly have continued to attend school on the off-chance that Ben Jones might award her another of his heart-stopping grins. Or even—O please, Goddess of Love!—a word. "Hi, Jess!" would do. She knew he was the strong silent type. Except in her daydreams, when he read her love poems, written by himself as the surf crashed all around them and the dogs playfully tried to pull off each other's Lycra shorts.

At lunchtime on Friday Jess and Flora sat on the bench in the science quad. Flora had lost her appetite. She could no longer do justice to the baguettes. She had also lost her appetite for conversation. Jess devoured her Mexican wrap. Flora toyed with a Greek salad. Suddenly Jodie bounced into view.

"Any room for me?" she asked. They made space and she plonked herself down. "Heard from lover boy?" she demanded. Flora blushed.

"No," she replied. "Well, not recently."

"Nor have I," said Jodie, taking a huge bite of a hot dog. "Never mind. Forget him. He's a waste of space. Have you heard about the school show at the end of next term? Apparently we can do comedy sketches as well as musical numbers and stuff. I think we should write something."

"Hmm," said Jess. She didn't want to commit herself. If she was going to write some comedy sketches it would have to be with Flora or Fred. Fred was back at school after several days off with a cold. His voice had gone deep like Shaggy. Fred had vowed never to go camping again in his entire life. He was such a nerd.

The bell went for afternoon school. Jodie got up and touched Flora briefly on the shoulder.

"Forget Gerard," she said. " 'No man is worth it,' as they say in *Some Like It Hot*." It seemed Jodie had got rid of her evil mood and was extending the olive branch. Jess felt relieved. It was good to be back in touch with Jodie's normal cheery self.

Flora, however, was so deeply depressed she could barely walk or talk. She dragged herself up off the bench and slouched off to maths. She would normally have trotted happily off to maths, like a puppy going on a walk.

After maths it was history, and then they walked home. Some of the time, Flora was actually crying, silently. As they neared her house she dried her eyes on a tissue.

"Come in with me, Jess," she pleaded. "I'll tell my mum I was crying about the execution of King Charles the First." They'd been studying that in history. It had been a fun afternoon.

Flora's mum was out at the hairdresser's, so no lying was necessary. They went up to Flora's room. She switched on her laptop and checked her e-mail. Nothing.

"He hasn't e-mailed me or texted me for over five days," she said. Her face was pale, her eyes huge and brimming. "I've sent him messages every day. What if he's been killed in an accident or something?"

Jess realized her time had come. Up till now, she hadn't wanted to tell Flora the truth because she knew it would destroy her happiness. Now she *had* to tell her because there was just a chance it would, ultimately, destroy her *un*happiness.

"OK," said Jess. "It's time you knew."

"Gerard is a flirt and a time-wasting womanizer," said Jess. She said it fast, so it might possibly hurt less. Flora looked shocked and panicky. Then she frowned and her eyes flashed.

"*What?*" she said.

"Just before he got with you on the camping trip, he was holding my hand and telling me how great I was," said Jess. "I didn't say anything when you and he got together because I didn't want to upset you. You seemed so happy and, well, I suppose I thought he was entitled to change his mind."

Flora looked troubled. You could tell hundreds of

thoughts were racing across her mind. But she said nothing, and her eyes were hostile.

"But then," Jess went on, "when we said goodbye on Saturday, he whispered something really gross in my ear and gave me his card and asked me to write to him."

"Something really gross?" gasped Flora. "What?"

Jess told her. Flora cringed and went pale, but she didn't look quite so tragic anymore. She was still hostile, but now the target was Gerard, not Jess.

"Don't cry," said Jess. "Jodie was right about one thing—he's not worth it."

"There'll be no more goddamn crying!" said Flora, though she was deathly pale. She picked up the jacket she'd just taken off, and put it on again. "I need to go for a walk," she said. "On my own for a bit. Sorry."

"It's fine, it's totally fine!" said Jess. "I have to go on home anyway. I've got heaps of stuff to do."

When she got home, Jess's first task was to clear out her pockets. She found the card Gerard had given her. On the back he had written, To dear Jess. Love Gerard, and there were three kisses. Jess stared at it thoughtfully for a couple of seconds, and then rather ceremoniously burnt it in a saucer.

"Goodbye forever, loser," she said. "You're not worthy to kiss the seat of my rather enormous pants."

Next day Flora was a different person. She was back to her old self. She bought a large baguette and took an enormous bite.

"God, it's such a relief to have my appetite back!" she said, through mouthfuls of egg mayo.

"And it's good to be able to talk properly again," said Jess.

"I mean, when we were camping, I couldn't communicate with you. It was horrible."

"I'm really sorry," said Flora thoughtfully. "It's weird how that happened."

"It's the story of my life," said Jess. "I can't talk to my mum about my dad, I can't mention my mum to my dad, my mum and dad can't talk to each other, my granny talks to dead people . . ."

"I can't talk to my dad either," said Flora. "I have to rehearse everything in my head before I speak to him."

"And for two weeks I was banged up with a Hobbit who only spoke Elvish," said Jess. "You were lucky, having Marie-Louise. She was great. Have you heard from her?"

"Yes," said Flora. "Apparently her boyfriend wasn't two-timing her. Although she still sounded a bit uneasy about it. I don't think she can really trust him."

"Men!" said Jess. "Hopeless. Can't talk, won't talk."

At this moment Fred swooped past them and did a mime as if lifting his hat politely in a 1940s film.

"Good day, ladies!" he said. "Can't stop! Have to save the world by two-thirty."

"There is Fred, of course," said Flora. "He never stops talking."

"Yes, of course, Fred," said Jess. "I can communicate with him. But he's so eccentric—he's a one-off."

There was a pause while they got on with their baguettes. Jess's was cheese and pickle. She could feel it going down her throat and heading straight for her hips.

"Have you still not heard from Gerard?" asked Jess. "Or is it a pointless question?"

"Oh no," said Flora bitterly. "And I hope I never do. I hate him now. It's great, actually. I feel kind of free, you know? But I am a bit guilty about you, Jess. I mean, he hit on me after he'd started with you, and you never said a thing. You must have been totally pissed off. It must have seemed like I'd grabbed your guy."

"Oh, it was no big deal," said Jess. "It wasn't like he'd proposed or anything. I didn't mention it because I didn't want to hurt you. Although, to be honest, there were moments when I wanted to murder you—painlessly, of course."

"You are the best friend in the galaxy," said Flora, "and may my fingernails be pulled out one by one if I ever dump all over you like that again."

"If we just make sure we always keep talking," said Jess, "nothing like this will ever happen again." She was to remember this conversation a couple of months later.

"OK," said Flora. "It's a deal. Now, we're through with live men, obviously, so I'm going to have a crush on someone who's already dead. Kurt Cobain, maybe, or River Phoenix. If he's already dead he can't two-time me, can he? Who are you going to have a crush on?"

A divine face hovered in Jess's imagination. She heard the dim, distant roar of a football crowd, she saw a shy smile, a cool crown of Californian blond lifeguard hair, a pair of baby blue eyes. Her heart gave an excited little jump, like a gerbil leaping for a piece of cheese.

"It's a secret," she said, smiling to herself. But she had a feeling that her secret crush on Ben Jones was bound to mutate into a full-scale melodrama in no time at all.

She just had to finish this baguette first.

About the Author

Sue Limb lives on an organic farm in a remote part of Gloucestershire. Her writing career has included various assignments for magazines and newspapers, radio work, television series, and several novels for adults published in Britain. Her books for children include *Big and Little, China Lee, Me Jane, Big Trouble, Mr. Loopy and Mrs. Snoopy,* and *Come Back, Grandma,* which was short-listed for the Smarties Prize. Sue's first novel about the charmingly crazed Jess Jordan, *Girl, 15, Charming but Insane,* is available from Delacorte Press.

Sue Limb is quite interested in gardening, travel, green politics, agriculture, and especially rare breeds of poultry, about which she is particularly mad.